Getting
to the
End

M I C H A E L   W I L L I S

PAGE PUBLISHING
Conneaut Lake, PA

First originally published by Page Publishing 2022

ISBN 978-1-6624-4484-5 (pbk)
ISBN 978-1-6624-4485-2 (digital)

Printed in the United States of America

I step out into the drizzling rain, trot to the car, and quickly slide into my seat while trying to remember if I've forgotten anything before my long trek to the office. Briefcase? Check. Eyeglasses? In my top pocket. Umbrella? On the floorboard. Coffee? In my hand. Anything else matters? Hmmm, not at the moment. Automatic morning ritual, don't want to get down the road and realize I forgot something…again!

Steering the car through the neighborhood, I make my way to take the interstate for the hour-long haul ahead. No other choice, I live on the outskirts of the greater Metro area, any faster way, believe me, I'd be on it. No need to rush, I got at least an hour, and that's on a good day. Mondays aren't ever good days! Stuck in traffic is certain most days. Sure, we considered buying closer to my work, but that would mean living in a heavily congested area, where even a quick trip to anywhere can be daunting. Thank God this is usually just a fleeting thought. The image of my back patio overlooking the pool quickly jumps into my brain. Add me with a nice glass of Four Roses—one cube—while taking in the sound of Brian Culbertson, Keiko Matsui, or that sultry voiced Anita Baker, well…that's all I need to quickly jerk me back to reality. Hell, I'd drive two hours each way to be able to avoid that congested city living…had that before and never did feel relaxed, even while at home. Damn, can we skip this week and fast forward to Friday? This has become my every Monday morning prayer, just never comes true!

My wife of forty years doesn't have this challenge anymore. Cecelia has the privilege and luxury of working from our home. Previously, she was a partner in one of the area's premier architectural firms when she decided it was time to go out on her own. As a freelance project consultant, she can now choose when she wants to work, not when someone else demands. Her specialty is landscape architecture and takes only projects with clients worth her time. This is ideal, especially since our two kids, now in their late thirties, have both been well-established on their own for some time. Jimmy and Olivia were born just two years apart. For the first several years of our marriage CeCe, as I refer to her affectionately, began as a part-time drafting specialist and a full-time mom. She studied architectural design in college, hoping to eventually prove herself in her own business at some point.

After the kids got a bit older, CeCe was hired by Davis & Smythe, and her career was kick-started into high gear. She progressed up the corporate ladder, eventually achieving partner status when Mr. Davis's health curtailed his full-time commitment. As a partner in this very busy and extremely successful business, CeCe had a ton of responsibility, regularly working long hours and bringing home her work on many occasions. She's definitely paid her dues and earned her badges, for sure. Needless to say, I was apprehensive when she approached me about going out on her own as female-owned business ventures, especially in the architectural field, don't typically have much success. No question, though; it was a major effort getting her business up and running that first year. However, she did it and has proven to be a great decision for both of us, financially as well as for our own sanity. This may be why we've lasted so long together, as we know several couples who've split with their significant others in recent years...maybe those significant others weren't so significant after all!

I was fortunate to have met CeCe back when we were in college together. And, I mean that—I literally found her when she wasn't looking for anyone at that time in her life. We were in the same English course together when I asked her if she had a spare pen, and it was on! Clearly, pursuing CeCe and winning her love could be the best decision I have ever made—no, it WAS the absolute best decision of my life. Right from the start, I knew she was special and I was determined to get her to notice me, even if it took me the whole semester—and it almost did! In addition to being an 8 or 9 on the scale of 1–10 (hey, no one gets to be a 10 unless you're primarily known by just one name like Sophia, Scarlett, Halle...you get the picture), Cecilia is a very sensitive and unique woman, not just because she's my wife, although I will admit it; I am prejudiced. Who wouldn't be? A woman like that just doesn't come around in a regular guy's life often. Nope; no, sir! The expression "she lights up the room when she enters," well, in my opinion, that fits her to a tee. But don't just take my word for it, everyone who meets her for the first time expresses that same feeling. She makes friends easily, has that honest, sincere, genuine outlook on life that's almost too innocent at times. Admittedly, I've had to deal with some inner demons called jealousy and insecurity in the past, almost to the detriment of completely blowing it a few times during our marriage. But she has always remained loyal and faithful to our union despite my petty worries. I have to say, I've been a lucky man, yes...a very lucky man indeed!

As I accelerate up the on-ramp onto the interstate, it occurs to me that there's something about starting a brand-new week that involves both regret and anticipation. Regret, due to the sobering reality that the weekend is officially over, and yet I can't help also feel a bit of anticipation as well. What will I face when I get into work today? Such is the norm for me as my primary job is dealing with the problems, concerns, and nonsense of other people. I really have no idea what others commonly refer to as a regular workday routine. There's certainly nothing, ABSOLUTELY NOTHING routine about my work; nope, no such luck. But to be completely honest, I think I kinda like it that way. Routine and regular sound very boring to me. Believe me, though, dealing with people and their problems—now THAT will never be boring! When I have to deal with something at work, the odds are it most likely started sometime over the weekend. This is what gives me that anxious feeling on Monday mornings. I don't know what it is about the weekends but while most sane people cherish and enjoy their weekend rituals, those with other motives in life—the full moon notwithstanding—seem to always get themselves twisted in ways you just can't even imagine or even anticipate. That's what makes my Monday mornings so interesting and full of anticipation…or dread! There's a common theme among my staff in our Monday morning meetings: what craziness will we encounter today? Kind of like the proverbial ticking time bomb, and of course, no clue as to when it will blow. Welcome to my world, the mother of all adult babysitting gigs! As sure as my name is William J. McCallister, Director of Human Resources for Ocean Direct, Inc., the largest seafood distribution company in the state. Seriously, stuff happens in my world at work that you just can't make up. And I am charged with dealing with it—or at least, trying to anyway—every single day, every week…so how did I get so lucky!

As I fall into line with the other commuters on the road, the events of the weekend filter through my mind. Getting together with close friends on Saturday night at Jack and Claire's house was great, as usual. By now, you might assume that I really look forward to my relaxation time away from work. And you would be so correct! The weekends with CeCe and our friends are my time to recharge, even if it's just for a while and never long enough. Of course, with one's friends, there can also be some stressful times. Charlie Mason, my closest friend from childhood and part-time golfing buddy, always seems to enjoy himself a little more than the rest of us. Alcohol plays a big part in that process for Charlie. Occasionally, he will innocently offend someone in our group, as he becomes quite opinionated the more alcohol he consumes. For the most part, we give Charlie Mason a pass when this happens as we learned a long time ago it's just easier than trying to convince a high-functioning alcoholic he's had too much to drink. Besides, his wife, Janie, keeps close tabs on him and signals the rest of us to redirect Charlie, as necessary. Only a few times have I had to take him home before the evening was over, only to hear him vent, threaten to kick my ass for forcing him into the car, and then tell me how much he loves me before collapsing onto his bed and sleeping it off for the rest of the night. Of course, not remembering anything at all the next day is par for the course! I will say, though, he does apologize profusely to whom he offends when he realizes he's guilty; maybe that's why we tolerate his behavior. Without question, Janie already has a special reservation in heaven. Anyone that can put up with Charlie like her surely has to be an angel. Other than that, he's a great guy!

Our close-knit group consists of five couples whom we've known for several years. Two couples—Charlie and Janie, and Mark and Debbie Feinstein—go back to our college days, and the other three are from CeCe's work connection. We're all around the same age, nearing that time in life where retirement plans begin to take center stage. Being all empty nesters and been there for a while, we make time to get together as a group. Charlie owns a dry-cleaning business he inherited from his family after his father passed away several years ago. Dave and Steph Sansone are the most recent addition to our group, and they are both on their second marriages. Dave is a Vietnam war vet and owns an airport limousine service. Steph Sansone is an RN critical care specialist at the local hospital. They are both very headstrong people and openly speak their minds. Makes for some stimulating conversation, however, also invariably serves as a catalyst for Charlie's input after he's had several whiskey sours. So you can easily imagine the spirited debate when the conversation turns to politics religion, or world affairs.

Jack and Claire, the oldest members of our social circle, enjoy entertaining, and they have quite the place to pull that off. They have a five-bedroom, two-story, brick-and-stone monster house in an upscale community with a huge outdoor patio, country kitchen, large backyard, and massive screened-in pool area perfect for entertaining multiple guests. Their home is extremely more luxurious than the typical dwellings of most other upper-middle-class people, where the rest of us reside. Jack was a software developer who made his fortune peddling his talents to the highest bidder back during the '80s Dot Com era. Obviously, as a founding pioneer, he did very well indeed. Claire and CeCe worked together at Davis & Smythe where they became real close friends. Each year, he trades his last year's model Maserati for the newest version as soon as it can be ordered, and without exception, Jack just has to show off his new prized possession—every year! It's an annual ritual, kind of like a special holiday event, so to speak. Oh, did I mention this happens EVERY year? They have no hesitation demonstrating their good fortune at every opportunity, but with one caveat—insisting we come to their house. They wouldn't have it any other way. Of course, both he and Claire are always quick to toss out other invitations for get-togethers, having no specific reason whatsoever. This past weekend was one of those events. Maybe that's why it was more enjoyable this time, everyone was relaxed and in good spirits…and I do mean good spirits! Surprisingly, even Charlie seemed to be on best behavior. I don't recall hearing about any misgivings on his part, at least not so far. But the week is still young!

As for my chosen career path, please don't misunderstand, I've thoroughly enjoyed it. It has been both challenging and rewarding, for the most part! Currently, I'm responsible for the general welfare and care of approximately 2,500 team members—not a simple task; no, sir! I've had the privilege of meeting and getting to know various interesting people from many different backgrounds and life experiences. This is exactly what I had imagined it would be when I started out to make my mark after graduation. My first job as employment manager for a small municipality was quite the learning curve for me, in the truest sense. Initially, I really struggled to try to understand the actions of the people who worked there—some behaviors just didn't make any sense to me! But in retrospect, I learned a lot from that first job, fresh out of school. Yes, I made several rookie mistakes, but it was a perfect place for my development. Good news is no one expects you to be top-notch; hey, what can I say, you work for the government. Even in city government, most people are there for life, and unless you steal something or have a major physical altercation with another coworker, you absolutely cannot get yourself fired. Yeah, I think that's an unwritten rule for working in any government position! I would throw in "sexual promiscuity" here, but given the recent events in the world of politics, I'm not sure this qualifies as an actual threat to job security any more.

I've always been a competitive person. Just give me a challenge, and I'm all over it. I learned a very long time ago that most successful corporate leaders prefer to promote and reward that "can do" attitude! They believe from own experiences that this is the best motivation for incentivizing the underlings as well. Any intern learns pretty soon that pleasing the boss will get them further than just showing up and doing the job. This almost goes without saying, especially when the expectation for a first-year, fresh-out-of-college newbie is not that high anyway. The really smart ones soon realize that if they also demonstrate initiative, resourcefulness, and the art of stepping on the back of their colleagues without detection to please the boss… then the future is there for the taking! Seasoned executives look for these specific key traits within their staff members who are labeled as "go-getters." This self-fulfilling practice in business is commonly referred to as obtaining "a notch in the gun belt" for those competing to develop the next bright star in the organization. For that executive believes the more they recognize, mentor, train, and develop talent for senior management approval, then their role in the pecking order is safe or so they believe. Everyone in the organization must impress—that's a standard requirement of corporate success and frankly essential to "protecting their phony-baloney jobs," to paraphrase a line out of the movie *Blazing Saddles*, starring Mel Brooks. From my perspective, it has always been amusing to see the interactions of middle management as they jockey for a position in the organizational pecking order. There have been times when the image of a Barnum & Bailey Circus act pops into my head, and that's putting it kindly! Surely, you're thinking I jest. Okay, but only if you think so!

Well, I'm painfully familiar with the expectation of "doing things right, the first time." It was instilled (*drummed* might be a better word!) into me right from the start with my father. Being the only son of a man who rose from having nothing but his word to the proud owner of a very successful hardware store in south Alabama, he expected and demanded absolute perfection, nothing else would ever be good enough! My father went through so many different employees at his beloved store, mostly post-high school kids who didn't possess either the aptitude or means to get into college. If he kept any of these poor souls on any longer than three months, I can't recall. How do I know this? Of course, I was expected to be there after school and on weekends when I was home from college on breaks and over the summers. I felt bad for the regular kids though; they were never going to survive my father's demanding work expectations. Christ, I barely survived, and I couldn't even quit! It's also something no son can possibly ever live up to, no matter how hard I tried and ultimately failed. Never mind that though; "No excuses… you should have done better," he would say. And it didn't even matter what it was. Working at the store, Little League baseball, junior varsity football, schoolwork, helping around the house, I could go on and on. There was no such thing as preferential treatment either; everything in his life as far as I was concerned revolved around making me be exactly like him. No son of Joe McCallister was ever going to do something half-assed or ever fail. Guess this was what initially gave me that drive to try to understand why people do what they do. It's precisely why I studied psychology in college; it's what piqued my interest in Human Resources. But thankfully, that is the past; my dad and I had more than patched up our differences well before he passed a few years ago. It was gratifying for me to know that the old man finally realized that I was capable of accomplishing something that even he could be proud of. I earned a college degree! This was a very significant step in our relationship since my father didn't get past the tenth grade as he was forced to drop out of school and go to work to provide for his mother and five siblings—something very common in families back in the post-Great Recession era if the primary breadwinner could no longer work. Unfortunately, my grandfather had endured a workplace accident that crippled and left him unable to continue to do his physically demanding job in the local cotton mill. Of course, another explanation for his late-in-life mellowness could be that my father just hit the wall and was too tired to continue trying to mold me in his image...but I'd really prefer to believe otherwise. He was very proud of me when I got that college degree—he would brag to the other old-timers who came into his store that his son, the CG (college graduate), as he would refer to me. However, I don't believe he would've been as equally proud of my antics—uhm, let me rephrase: "Charlie's and my antics" while we were away at college. Hey, Charlie was my best friend, and of course, he was a major influence on me. That's my story, and I'm sticking to it! Thank God, Mom and Dad never knew everything we did in our younger years! Come on, we all have something we're glad the parents never knew about—it was the seventies, for Christ's sake!

As a general rule, I make it a point to seek, hire, and promote those who demonstrate that same "can do" work ethic—that determined focus to do whatever is necessary to get the job done! I can't help it; old habits are hard to overcome. And then, always doing your absolute best to get to the top. I think it was Ralph Waldo Emerson who opined, "it's not the destination, it's the journey." You know, I really didn't understand exactly what that meant when I first read it. To me, the goal has always been getting results; didn't matter how you got there. Who the hell cares about the journey? But as I eventually learned along the way, evidently 'ole Waldo was right on—no truer statement could be more appropriate. To his point, everything in life has a price, but the one thing that can't be purchased is time. If you waste your time on the unimportant, then you've wasted your journey. Sadly, I don't think many people learn this until later in life, if they ever do. I just wish I had learned it a lot earlier than I did… no regrets, just sooner.

HR work has been very good to me. As proof of my success, I've been well-compensated—a competitive salary, good bonus potential, great 401(k) program, and even stock options for when I retire. Retirement? Well, I'm inside of two years until I take the road of not being a member of the full-time working class any longer. In my opinion, it couldn't come any sooner. I just hope I can make it…as there are times, usually Monday mornings, I wonder if I will! As I near the end of my career, I have to say that it has been both interesting and frustrating at the same time. I've accepted and certainly have no issue that people come in very different styles, types, versions— hell, pick a word here. You see, if I've learned anything from my work experiences, it's that people have vastly different ideas on what is acceptable both in and out of the workplace. Many Americans possess this innate desire to be different from everyone else based on their culture, race, gender, sexual preference, physical challenges, etc., and that also carries over into the workplace. We want to have our own identity, personality, make a distinct mark on the world, and be unique. Nothing wrong with any of that; it's what's makes us who we are. But it is my firm belief that it is the company's responsibility to define the parameters by which behavior is to be governed and accepted in the workplace and educate/train team members on those rules. Obviously, it just doesn't always go as expected especially when it's essential that everyone must work together in harmony. Too much productivity is forever lost when you have a dysfunctional workplace whether that be due to a single employee, an incompetent manager, or the organization's lack of recognition or refusal to admit the problem. Successful managers want employees to perform as a team—obviously best for getting the work done effectively and efficiently which should be a primary goal. But when personalities and cultures clash, that's when the potential for problems arises. Sometimes these problems are not so easy to determine or detect. Generally, most people know when they should've said something to a coworker in a better way. When behavior crosses the line in the workplace, the HR department plays a critical role in dealing with it. After all, human emotion is not relative to education, experience, or judgment. Whether it's perpetrated by an entry-level employee or a long-term top-level executive, when it comes to expressing one's opinion, human emotion does not relate to the amount on the paycheck…(Sh)it just happens! I've certainly had to deal with my share of "executive misbehavior" as well. Human emotion is the one thing that we HR people are required to deal with, even when it originates outside the organization.

The human resource professional, a vitally important position of high integrity and keeper of the company's deepest and darkest secrets—probably the most respected person in the organization. When HR speaks, everyone listens! Wait, that's E. F. Hutton, uh sorry…got carried away there for a moment. HR work sounds exciting though…right? Ha! As the ranking leader in the HR discipline for my company, unfortunately, I'm more like a referee between a bunch of spoiled rotten and entitled millennials and an overly judgmental and critical group of aging baby-boomer management. My primary role, as I see it, is to try and keep the peace, or as they officially call it in HR circles, "conflict resolution." Fortunately, not everyone or everything I deal with fits into this category; however, because it is usually urgent, that always takes priority. Honestly, maybe I've already seen my best years, past my prime, as they say, but one thing is for sure, if you don't balance your personal and work life together, no matter what type of work you do, you will not last long. In the HR function, without balance, you will burn out quickly. I've literally seen that happen to some of my colleagues. HR work mostly centers around those few employees who have issues, problems, disagreements, needs, questions, and concerns. This routinely involves only about 10 percent of the workforce. The other 90 percent generally just come to work, do their jobs, and never seem to bother anyone else. As a matter of fact, as an HR person, you have to make a specific effort to interact with those who fall into this category. They rarely come to the HR office, and they surely don't require much attention. Jack Welch, former chairman of General Electric was often quoted as saying that leaders should fire the bottom 10 percent of their workforce each year. Something he defended as absolutely necessary to improve the organization and vehemently argued that all companies should incorporate the 10 percent rule. Obviously, Jack was certainly old-school in his strategic business thinking, but then again, maybe he was actually onto something. No question, it can be overwhelming at times…if you let it!

Speaking specifically about cultural differences, in my experience, this seems to be a major obstacle for people being able to coexist peacefully in the workplace. Even senior-level, long-term, well-educated, highly intelligent executives have their cultural biases. Case in point, at a previous place of employment several years ago, I had befriended a fellow coworker who was in charge of our accounting department. Joe and I hit it off almost immediately right after he joined the firm. We just seemed to have several things in common, including our love of college football and the sweet taste of good bourbon on occasion. He and I frequently shared lunch together, spending the time to discuss many different topics. Even though we had many similarities—ex-athletic endeavors, fishing, and golf—we did have some differences, but it seemed like they were unimportant to either one of us at the time. In addition, his wife and CeCe got to know each other through the four of us having dinner together, and they scheduled their own personal time for coffee and shopping on occasion. We even had them join us from time to time with our special friends on weekends. Jack and Claire and the group welcomed them both warmly, and it seemed like everything couldn't be better having their friendship as close as it was.

Then, it happened…Joe, this person I really liked a lot but really didn't know for very long at all, said something that changed our relationship forever, in many ways. We were at lunch one day, and he made a degrading comment about the Black waitress who seemed to be having a rough day. She didn't smile at all and let's just say her tableside manner wasn't the best. Her guest service skill was totally absent that day; perhaps she had other more important events going on in her life that prevented her from being her best. Since this was a frequent lunch spot, I was sure she had waited on us previously and we never had any issue. However, when she dropped off the check this time, she didn't even look at us or give the customary server closing, "Thank you for coming in today, if there's anything else I can get you, please let me know. We appreciate your business." Even a simple "thank you" would have been the least she could have said. In any event, like most, I've had lousy service from others that was less than expected but this particular event was certainly not the worst.

After she had turned and started to walk away, Joe made a comment that shocked me and was uncharacteristic coming from him up until then. He said, "Wow, that Black hoe sure seemed to have her panties in a wad today, huh?"

Well, not only did hit me like a shot out of the dark, she apparently heard it as well as she turned her head around and gave him a scowl that only Clubber Lane would make right before he knocked the snot out of his opponent. Clubber was the fictional name of the boxing opponent for Rocky in the infamous *Rocky III* movie, played by "Mr. T." Needless to say, the glare from her was not pretty! Now, it's not that I haven't heard disparaging remarks about Black people or women or others of different persuasions before. Sadly, in my HR career, I've been involved in several employee disputes where inappropriate names and/or comments about another's heritage were said in anger and some even in hurtful fun. Obviously, as a company leader and the HR director, I've addressed those instances in support of not only the company policy but my own personal feelings as well. There is absolutely no place for hateful ugly remarks or name-calling whether in the workplace or not. This is something that has zero tolerance in my book.

So when Joe made this comment, and after taking a moment to collect myself, I said to him, "Joe, that wasn't appropriate and what's even worse, she heard you what—"

Before I could even finish, he came back with, "Oh, I see...you have your HR hat on. I thought we were just having a friendly lunch. I didn't know I was going to be judged as if I was on the clock." He sarcastically complained and there was no smile on his face.

All righty then, I'm thinking. *He wants to go down this road, let's roll.* "Joe, please don't misunderstand me. I don't have my HR hat on here. I don't like your comment as a person; and I think it's degrading to hear that coming from a leader in our company and even more so from you, someone I consider a close friend."

He just looks at me for a couple of moments and then shakes his head. "Well, you are certainly entitled to your opinion, Bill, but please don't lecture me on my choice of words. Besides, who anointed you the appropriate comment police?" And with that, he got up and left the table.

Since I had driven us both to lunch that day, I felt sure he was just going outside to cool down, so I fished out the correct amount for our meals and slowly finished my coffee. I got up and headed to the men's room to wash up, giving Joe more time to reflect on what he said, hoping he would reconsider what he said to me. However, when I went outside to the car, Joe was nowhere to be seen. I went around the building and walked up and down the parking lot, still no sight of him whatsoever. When I returned to the office, which took about fifteen minutes, I went directly to his office and there he sat, picking away on his desktop computer. At first, I was a bit surprised to see him since as I had no idea how he had beat me back to the office.

He looked up and said in a matter-of-fact way, "Bill, it's best if we don't talk right now. I'm in no mood to be chastised for what I said at lunch. You have your opinion and I have mine, it's better if we just drop the subject."

"Okay, Joe," I said. "It's your call for now, but at some point, we're gonna need to talk about this, eventually. It's not going away." And then I turned and walked away, giving him an opportunity to reflect.

I couldn't help but think that this was going to be a major divide in our relationship as his defense of the comment bothered me even more than what he had said. It just did not sit well with me, but I had a distinct feeling that this was going to be a real issue with us. As it was, Joe and I were never the same from that day forward. We stopped going to lunch together, and while he was cordial whenever we were in the same room, it was obvious that he still harbored ill feelings and that was uncomfortable for both of us. Now, I'm not the type to hold a grudge or continue hard feelings against someone over a disagreement. However, a fundamental difference such as this is a major problem for me, and this event with Joe just did not make any sense to me, at least at first. Ultimately, it became clear to me why this event occurred, and Joe's strange reaction to me calling him out.

Within the next few months, there was another situation at work that involved Joe and a team member who worked in the accounting department. This employee just happened to be Black and had been with ODI for almost ten years—five years longer than Joe. Joe had inherited him when he came on board, and even though the team member had good performance reviews prior to Joe's arrival, he had stagnated for the last five years while under Joe's supervision. Then one day, a member of my staff mentioned that the team member had come to see her complaining he had been passed over for a promotion for which he should have been next in line to get. He told her that Joe had told him he did not possess the right background for the promotion. Therefore, this employee believed he had been a target of discrimination. Now, I'm not saying that every employee who thinks they've been a victim of discrimination believes this because they have definitive proof; some just have a feeling they weren't treated fairly. However, if it seems like "where there's smoke, there could be fire," as the old saying goes, it's up to the organization to investigate. I suspected there might be some relevancy, so after discussing the matter with my boss and relaying the lunch event I had with Joe earlier, I was directed to proceed with looking into the matter. After all, I did not want to start an investigation on Joe that could be labeled a "witch hunt" due to the altercation I had with him previously.

As it turned out, our investigation found that Joe had clearly discriminated against this minority team member in his department, and there were other suspiciously related circumstances in the five years Joe had been on board. Some minority employees were moved into lateral positions that were either dead-end jobs or relegated to performing work beneath their qualified capabilities, even though they were compensated to perform work of a higher nature.

Following the intensive investigation in Joe's department, after several minority employees had given written statements to HR about how they felt like they were not seriously considered for any of the open positions for which they had applied, Joe was terminated. But what was most disturbing for me was that from the investigation, it was confirmed that Joe had not only openly discriminated against deserving minority team members, he actually mentioned that he was a close friend of the HR director whenever someone objected to his decision. The inference being, "Since I am friends with the HR director, you will have no case." This was not only a major turn of events for his department, it was a huge learning experience for me. I had blindly trusted someone with my friendship only to find out that we really did not share the same fundamental belief that everyone deserves to be measured and given a fair opportunity based on their abilities and efforts and not on the color of their skin. To make matters worse, I had put myself in a position of being taken advantage of—and I didn't even know or realize it.

It goes without saying, I was reluctant to trust anyone else going forward in my career with my friendship. Also knowing that I may be involved in disciplinary action could jeopardize that friendship later. I think many HR professionals have this experience during their tenure; it's part of that ugly side of human nature.

For the last five years, I've worked hard to develop my team of high-functioning professionals in preparation for my exit from the company. I like to think I've done everything possible to train and educate each one of them to be self-sufficient and stand on their own—they are a good group of individuals. Loyal, dedicated, focused, and the bottom line is that they really care about what they're doing. I've been blessed to have accumulated such a competent, humble, and easy-to-work-with group. And they make my life and the department better as they are highly respected by senior management as well as the rank-and-file employees. If I admit to one personal regret in my career, I'd say that I should have made the time to pursue that law degree. Not just for the money, necessarily, but to also enhance my skill set and complete one of my personal goals. Having worked with attorneys in the employment and labor law arena, I can honestly say that my knowledge from that experience has provided me with the knowledge and answers to many legal questions along the way. I think I would've made a good corporate lawyer, which could have set me up for a lucrative consulting opportunity. Ah, the possibilities… but over the past ten years, it wasn't a priority as Cecilia was getting her consulting business up and running during this time. For me to take away from that to improve my career ambitions would have been in conflict with hers, so I have no regrets at all. The end of my career will be here before I realize it, hopefully!

Who is going to aggravate me today? I wonder. Glancing at my watch and recognizing where I am, I realize I'm only a couple of miles from my exit and about ten minutes from the office. I landed this senior-level role reporting to the CEO about fifteen years ago when I answered a blind ad from a private search firm specializing in corporate assignments. Now, as I near the stepping-off place in my career, I wonder if I've really made a difference in some people's lives, have I done more good than bad with my decisions? Obviously, I'd like to believe that…but who really knows for certain?

Whoa! What! Where is this car going? Geeze, it's coming into my lane! Holy shit, it's a guy texting on his cell phone! HONK! HOOOONK. "You dumb ass," I mutter as he yanks his car back to the right! Where the hell is a cop when you need one? Why do we even have a law if it's not going to be enforced?

I glance over as I pass in the left lane. *Oh, okay. Nice one, ace. Flip me the bird…that's real intelligent. What a jerk!*

I just wave to the idiot as if I appreciate him getting his car out of MY lane. No sense in perpetuating a road rage incident on Monday. Jesus, I can't wait to be enjoying that better life. Can we fast forward two years from now? Please!

Upon arriving at work, coming through the side door, I turn into the outer office, and I immediately see our HR receptionist, stout and portly Rose Davis. "Good morning, Mr. McCallister! How was your weekend?"

"Rosie" is one of those extremely positive souls who is rarely in a bad mood, no matter what. The sky could be filled with meteors torching everything as they fell, but she would be saying, "Wow, look how beautiful the sky lights up!" Which is exactly why she was the quintessential receptionist for a department whose overall purpose of serving employees is priority number one. Her bubbly personality and boundless energy are great assets for us, as nothing good would come otherwise. Employees don't usually take time to come to the HR office to proclaim how much they love their job, their boss, or the company, that's for sure!

"Good morning, Rosie. The weekend is always too short," I mouth and smile broadly without breaking stride.

"Oh, Mr. McCallister, you're so right," she giggles.

As I walk past my staff seated in cubicles working my way toward my office, our employee relations manager, Sarah Jenkins, steps from her office apologizing for grabbing me first thing but asks if I have a few minutes to discuss a major situation. Crap, ten more feet and I would've made it to the sanctuary of my office and at least getting that first cup of aged office coffee before I was unwittingly corralled…damn! It's Monday morning, what else is new!

"Sure, of course. Good morning, Sarah!" I respond. For an instant, my mind is wondering if this might involve a warehouse employee named Alice Randle. This was quickly confirmed as I pass by our department conference room before ducking into my office. There, through the window, I see Alice sitting at the table with her head hanging down, hands folded on the table looking as if her world was about to end. Alice had been promoted to her new position of assistant warehouse director not more than six months ago. However, every couple of weeks since taking on her new role, there has been something involving her that has made it into our office. Obviously, this was going to be another related matter.

Sarah stepped into my office quickly closing the door behind her. "You will not believe what's going on with Alice Randle this time!" Sarah was generally the calm, easygoing, rational-headed professional—a perfect fit to handle employee relations problems. She is rarely bothered nor emotional about employee issues even though she has handled her fair share of some of the strangest and controversial situations you could ever imagine happening in the workplace.

Whenever there's a diverse group of people all together in close quarters, such as a work environment, there's always the potential for conflict of some sort. It's just human nature, and that's exactly why most human resources departments exist today…not the only reason, but it is a major responsibility. In order to adequately handle these conflicts today, which are too common in the workplace, someone must have the responsibility of monitoring morale and quickly resolving employee issues in a fair and impartial manner. Otherwise, overly opportunistic and litigious labor attorneys are just waiting to pounce on unresolved employee dissatisfaction and just a phone call away. Therefore, every prudent and bottom-line focused organization must have competent professional people on staff to address these matters…with the additional goal of minimizing legal fees and settlements. Otherwise, challenges in your organization can explode very quickly, morale will erode, and business costs will skyrocket due to ongoing employment dysfunction. Yes, I know, this sounds like I'm justifying the importance of the HR function in the company to a group of senior decision-makers tasked with making arbitrary payroll reductions. Believe me, I have been there, done that!

While barely into her forties, Sarah is a bright, energetic professional, possessing a strong ambition and solid work ethic that belies her youth and the sign of the times. She is able to quickly and thoroughly resolve conflict and employee concerns when challenged. She is extremely competent and gifted at resolving a case if she has been given accurate information. Forced to put her personal life on hold, she struggled through some extremely difficult personal issues as a Black woman to obtain her bachelor's degree. I had absolutely no problem recommending her for our company's fast track program four years ago. With ODI's financial assistance, she has been able to take advantage of continuing her education and pursue a master's degree in business administration. Sarah has been the ideal poster child for the success of our company's fast track program. Without a doubt, our senior management team clearly believes Sarah is the best and a legitimate replacement for me whenever I leave. That is…if I really make it to the end…mentally intact? We'll see, but don't think THAT hasn't crossed my mind on more than one occasion! In the ten years Sarah has been with ODI, I've grown to respect her insight and her opinion on employee matters as she is extremely insightful when it comes to recognizing different perspectives and weighing the facts to get to a conclusion. She clearly understands there are usually two sides to every story. Her knowledge of labor law is solid, she is an extremely compassionate listener, and most people find her delightfully approachable. I promoted her to the role of ERM two years ago, which was very well-deserved, and I consider her a most valuable asset. However, today, something is off with Sarah. She is obviously unusually shaken and bothered by something she needs to discuss regarding Alice Randle.

Sarah begins by saying Alice was already waiting for her when she arrived this morning just after seven-thirty. Alice was sobbing uncontrollably about a threat she had received, which she believes came from another employee. Alice told her she heard a knock on her door at home last night around 9:00 p.m., and when she opened the door, there was no one there. That's when she noticed there was an envelope sitting on the step of her porch. She leaned over, picked up the envelope, and written across the top was her name in red ink, Alice Randle, and the word, WHORE. Alice said she then walked out onto her lawn and looked all around up and down the street but didn't see anyone, and when she opened the envelope, she found a typewritten note, also written in red. Alice handed Sarah the note which read:

> Everybody knows how you got your job. YOU SLEPT WITH YOUR BOSS! If you do not resign immediately, you dirty whore, the proof of this will be sent to Mr. Johnson's office. Then we'll see how long you keep your job. YOU HAVE BEEN WARNED!

Sarah said she asked Alice if she might know who may have done this. Alice says she has no proof, but she is almost certain it came from one of her supervisors. She thinks it has to be from one of them because she doesn't believe they respect her at all because she is a woman. She knows they're not happy about her being promoted to the assistant warehouse director position and doesn't believe anyone else who works in the department would leave a note like this. Why would anybody leave this hurtful note on her doorstep…at her home! Sarah said she asked Alice why someone would accuse her of sleeping with Mr. Milken? Alice claims she has never been intimately involved with Mr. Milken. He is married, and she doesn't date married men. "My God, he's my father's age!" Sarah repeats Alice's exact comment. Obviously, she doesn't want to quit or lose her new job, so she thought someone in HR should know about this.

"Okay, Sarah, obviously appears like we have someone in the warehouse not happy about Alice getting the promotion. We knew this wasn't going to be popular with some who didn't get the job, but what are your thoughts?"

Sarah reminds me that we received several unsubstantiated written comments placed in the employee suggestion box that Alice has been flirting with some of the males out there. Sarah then tells me that Alice also mentioned that someone has been leaving some disturbing messages on her work voice mail saying she should quit because she did not deserve the promotion and dumb whores don't know how to be in charge of a group of men. She didn't come forward before because she couldn't identify who left these messages as they were done in a muffled tone. Initially, she even thought it might be some of her close friends playing a prank on her. Alice told Sarah that she had mentioned to a couple of close friends that she really enjoyed working for John Milken, her new boss because he treated her nice. But when she got the job, she heard that there were rumors going around in the warehouse about her and Mr. Milken, but she didn't think much of it. She knew that some of the "good 'ole boys" didn't think she was the best choice. Her friends, who liked to play crazy jokes on each other, teased her about how she might have "really earned" the promotion? Therefore, she didn't take the voice mails seriously as she thought her friends were just messing with her. Then starting last week, the voicemails became more hurtful and threatened that if she did not quit her job soon, she would regret it.

Sarah followed up with the question, "Alice, why didn't you come to HR sooner about all this?" All Alice would say is she knows now she should've.

Now, workplace violence and the threat of harm isn't something ODI has had any previous history of, even though it has become a real issue in some organizations. Of course, we've had to deal with the occasional profanity directed at another employee and the very rare threat of "I'm gonna knock your teeth out" type of comment, but this was something entirely new. One of ODI's Standards of Expected Employee Behavior is the respectful treatment of all fellow coworkers, and we have zero tolerance for violence and threats of violence on company premises. This had been ingrained in place way before I even came to work at ODI and has been consistently restated and signed off on every year along with every employee's annual review. Clearly, Sarah was bothered about this conversation with Alice and was unsure about what we should do about the matter. I assured her that we will get to the bottom, and based on what we know now, it needs to be a top priority definitely warranting a thorough investigation. We'll need to determine the validity of the threat and then who is the likely person this might be coming from. I asked her to get me the list of all the candidates that were being considered for the assistant director position before Alice was promoted. I'll confer with our outside legal counsel on the note and inform the CEO, Mr. Johnson, right away. I knew I didn't need to remind her, but I asked Sarah to document her conversation with Alice and to thank her for bringing the matter to us, letting her know that she did the right thing. In addition, we may need more information in the future but, for now, she should not mention any of this to anyone as it is now an active investigation for which we have to follow a specific protocol.

I asked Sarah to contact the IT department to have the voice mails pulled from her desk phone to download and secure them for the investigation. Sarah asked if we should get our security office involved at this point.

"Well, under normal circumstances we would have the security team take the lead on this matter, but due to the situation, I think it best to keep it here in HR for now. I'd like to inform Mr. Johnson first and let's take it from there," I said. So, this will be today's Monday morning catastrophe for the human resources department today. Welcome to the new work week!

John Milken is the director of distribution for the warehouse and has served in that role for the past twenty-two years. He worked his way up from forklift driver when he was hired into ODI more than thirty-five years ago after leaving the Marines. While serving in the Marines, he rose to the rank of staff sergeant in his ten years in the military and was involved in three tours of Vietnam, being discharged under, okay, let's say, curious circumstances. His military records have been sealed, however; he did receive an honorary discharge, as proven by a copy in his ODI personnel file. John claims his records are sealed because he was involved in a secret mission that if the details were known to the public, he could become a target—target of who? Who knows, only John knows, and he ain't telling.

In his position here at ODI, he is responsible for more than 350 full-time employees including delivery drivers, forklift operators, and warehouse personnel with a staff of twelve subordinate leaders called area supervisors. He has worked every position in the warehouse and therefore, knows everything that goes on in there. No one could ever put one past John or risk the embarrassment of being called out for it. He has a reputation of being hardnosed and gruff, and worst of all, he does not want anyone getting into his business in warehouse operations, especially HR. John is solely responsible for staffing his team with mostly those who resemble himself—a good ol' boy from the south side where pickup trucks, country cookin', and beer drinkin' are the primary topics of discussion. Not that there's anything wrong with any of this, but to avoid placing women into positions for which they are quite qualified to do based on their gender is not only wrong, it's illegal.

The area supervisors or ASs as they are called collectively and tongue-in-cheek affectionately by the employees in the warehouse cover three shifts around the clock, seven days a week. The assistant distribution manager position was created because of the growing workload in the warehouse due to the increase in demand from retailers for our client's seafood products. In order to avoid the perception of a series of continual unfairness with job promotions, the new job was posted internally with general qualifications for those who might be interested.

Far too long, hiring for the staffing for warehouse operations has been considered unfair, which has been mostly current employees recommending friends for open positions and that led to a makeup of almost all young White males. In the past, it was typical for most open positions to be filled based on personal recommendation and not always posted internally for current employees to apply. For many years, John and the warehouse management staff believed that warehouse work was best suited for young men due to the physical requirements. Consequently, any open position beyond entry-level semi-skilled work was filled from within of those who were already on board, and that included the forklift operator position. That all changed in the last few years as more women began entering the work force. And the forklift operator position is hardly a physical job; it just requires a certification and manual dexterity which a woman could certainly perform with absolutely no trouble. However, this was met with defiant resistance from John and his supervisor group, until I informed our CEO of the potential liability of ODI not having female representation in positions such as forklift operator jobs. Mr. Johnson, the CEO, agreed, and we developed plans with specific efforts to hire women into the warehouse and forklift operator openings, which is how Alice Randle came to be an employee. Needless to say, this did not sit well with the good ol' boy network, and John Milliken was quite vocal about his displeasure with this new hiring initiative. It came down to a showdown between John and the HR department, and when the CEO sided with HR, John had no option but to reluctantly accept the directive. Behind the scenes, he was less than enthusiastic to say the least, and he tried everything possible to circumvent the process, even citing every little failure of any woman working in the warehouse. This went on for several months until John and I wound up in the CEO's office with the senior VP of operations, Sam Morris, John's boss. There was a heated exchange about the matter, to say the least. Obviously, we know who won that battle, but it has always been a bone of contention between John and myself, straining our working relationship to the point where he tries to deliberately avoid the HR department at every opportunity. Of course, areas like training, wage and benefit administration, and employee relations are just a few of the areas where HR has to be involved to be consistent with our company standards and programs. It has been a challenge, but having Sarah be the liaison from HR to the warehouse has helped make this connection work. Bottom line, we have to work together, but we don't have to like it…or each other.

Fast forward to two years ago, Alice had been promoted to a supervisor's position in the box-making department, over John Milken's objection. But he saw this as a safe move since 90 percent of the employees working in this division of the warehouse were female, and she was well-qualified, having been a forklift operator and lead person in that area. What John did count on or expect was that Alice improved the box-making function so well and to the point she was solely responsible for a major cost savings initiative that saved ODI several hundred thousand dollars in just six months. When the decision to add the assistant general manager position to the warehouse was made, Mr. Johnson strongly felt that Alice should be included in with the other supervisor candidates based on her job performance as supervisor in the box-making department. It also would solve another glaring issue we had as a company by considering a female for a key decision-making role, especially in the warehouse. We had made some recent significant progress in promoting and hiring females into key positions in other areas of the company but not so much in the warehouse.

As the process went, Mr. Johnson became adamant that it would be in ODI's best interest to place a female into the assistant distribution manager position, the last bastion of male dominance in the company. This was also just after we had a female employee challenge a promotion she did not get in our sales department. Obviously, this matter being fresh in our CEO's mind; he did not want a similar problem occurring in an area of the company we could hardly defend as even moderately diverse. Alice was the only female supervisor in our warehouse operations at that time. However, there were some senior management concerns voiced that Alice may not have enough supervision experience, specifically in any other areas of the warehouse to be a legitimate candidate for the newly created assistant general manager role. However, none of the other ASs had supervised in other areas of the warehouse operations, either, even though they had been in their positions longer than Alice. John made his wishes known and lobbied hard for one of his longtime male supervisors. However, this fell apart when the guy insulted a female employee by claiming she needed to wear a larger bra because her boobs were bulging out on the side of her blouse. He removed his name from consideration for the new job after the matter was referred to HR, and he was reprimanded for his comments. We later learned that John claimed secretly to his staff that he believed the woman purposely wore the wrong-sized bra based on advice from HR just to trap his chosen man for the new job.

Unbelievable! Gives you an idea exactly what I've been up against with John and his team of supervisors and their shenanigans. He expects his supervisors to toe the line, follow his orders to the letter, and avoid unnecessary contact with HR, or else they will be on the outside looking in. He does not want top management, specifically his boss, HR, and the CEO to hear about any employee issues coming from the warehouse. Accordingly, John always tells me everything was going just great in the warehouse whenever we crossed paths in management meetings, even if I wasn't even asking that question. Definitely gave me the impression he did not want HR snooping around his department looking for something that was or wasn't there.

Initially, following Alice's promotion, it did not take long for rumors and gossip mostly behind the scene to surface. Most employees, especially the male supervisors, began talking that Alice must have been personally involved with John to get the promotion, since she did not have as long a tenure in the warehouse as the others. To further support this general feeling among those who did not agree with Alice getting her new job, she was a divorced mother of two, about fifteen years younger than John, and she made a striking appearance, especially when she wore tight clothing. John Milken was in his midsixties, married, with grown children and grand kids. He was generally introverted, not always a politically correct, and a workaholic, often spending extra hours on the job, especially during the busy season around the holidays. Typical of an old-school kind of manager, he had no problem with putting in the time whenever he felt like it was required. And it was widely speculated that John's wife could not care less about this since John was more of a kick-ass-and-take-names type manager on the job and most likely had that same demeanor at home as well. At a company Christmas party five years ago, she made a comment to the group at their table that she always looked forward to the holiday season when she could always count on John working extra hours. You can read between the lines there.

Alice, being a friendly likable woman, apparently enjoyed joking and teasing especially when it came to conversations with the males, which, while not inappropriate in the workplace, was nonetheless a practice that was questionable in her new role. She was now supervising males exclusively, and several of them did not think highly of her anyway. Until now, there had not been any formal complaints about Alice's behavior, but there were some anonymous comments reported to HR through the company suggestion program. Sarah, my ERM, coordinated the employee suggestion program, and in her conversations about the comments with John, she had informed him of the suggestions that were showing up about Alice. He had agreed to discuss the matter with her at his first opportunity, but it now appears like that never actually happened. As part of her questioning about the letter, Sarah had asked Alice if John had ever spoken to her about these anonymous suggestions coming into HR regarding her joking and being overly friendly with the male employees. Alice vehemently denied that he had ever said anything and stated that she did not do anything inappropriate like that at all—ever!—but did admit she was always friendly with everyone, including women employees, and because she was not married, she was sure some of the other women did not care for her talking to the male employees, even though some of them did the very same thing all the time. Hmmm, must be a woman kind of issue…

Okay, it's only been forty-five minutes, and I've been brought up to speed on the continuing saga of Alice Randall in the warehouse. I'm now on my way to bring the CEO in the loop before I reach out to Dave Mosier, our labor attorney, to get his initial thoughts about the letter Alice found on her front step.

As I make the short walk to Carl Johnson's office, I run smack into our senior vice-president of operations in the hall, apparently on his way to see me, who then asks if I was aware that Alice Randle has been getting threatening voice mails at work. What? I just found this out not ten minutes ago, how does Sam Morris know about this already? Talk about a vibrantly active rumor mill!

"Sam, I'm on my way now to Carl's office to bring him up to speed, you're welcome to join in the discussion."

To which Sam says, "Carl already knows about it, we were discussing it a little while ago."

All right, I'm thinking to myself, *so where's the leak?* Is it someone in my office or is Alice running around telling everyone about this before she came to HR this morning?

Sam says he received a phone call from John Milliken about an hour ago, and he mentioned the voice mails, which, of course, he informs Carl because of who this involves.

"Okay, Sam, suppose you let me know what you know before I go into to see Carl. I don't want to waste his time or get blindsided if he already knows all about this matter."

Sam just says that all he knows is that John called him and told him that someone has been sending in complaints to the HR department saying Alice is flirting with male employees in the warehouse and now she's getting threatening calls on her voice mail saying she better resign.

"Bill, did we make a huge mistake promoting that woman to the assistant general manager's job? If she's not capable of handling the position and behaving inappropriately then this isn't going to be good for that whole operation, you know that. Besides, where there's smoke there's usually fire, and I think we have several other options for that role. Sorry, Bill, gotta run. Another meeting. We'll talk later," Sam quips as he hurries off before I could respond.

Oh brother, I'm thinking. *See how distorted a little information can be when rumors are rampant about people and situations? We most definitely have our work cut out for us on this one! That could be the understatement of the year!* Little did I know, at that moment, it was about to get extremely complicated—and soon!

As I walk into the outer office of Carl Johnson, our CEO, I'm greeted by his executive admin assistant, Jayne Davis.

"Good morning, Mr. McCallister," she says without even looking up. "Mr. Johnson is expecting you, go right on in."

"Thank you, Jayne, and good morning to you too. I hope you had a nice weekend," I mumble, not really expecting a response.

"Why, it was very nice, sir, and I hope yours was pleasant too?" she responded. Jayne was one of the bright spots in our organization. She was the consummate professional administrative assistant, always on top of everything and everyone. She was more than just a right hand to whoever she worked with, she was also very bright, and her value to the organization was way beyond her role. But of course, Johnson wasn't going to have just anyone in this key role. He had me search high and low for the best of the best, and we went through more than twenty-five very well-qualified candidates before he settled on Jayne as his choice. In my opinion, anyone of the top six finalists would have been a good choice, and I consider myself a very picky hiring manager. However, Jayne has continually proven herself to be the best choice we could've made many times over in her four years of service…even if we did pay more than one-and-a-half times the going rate to get her on board. But great fit and great results aren't always easy to find, and Jayne fills both of those of those demands so we pay her more…okay, a lot more!

"Morning, boss, hope your weekend went well?" I said, announcing my presence, noticing that he has his head down engrossed in something obviously important.

"Yes, good morning, Bill. I'll be with you in a sec, have a seat," he mutters, without looking up.

Scanning his office while I wait to get his attention, I see he has added more golf paraphernalia to his already large collection on display. Carl is an avid golfer who plays several times a week and is quite good at it, I might add. He has been the club champion for his country club for the past three years running, evidenced by the trophies and plaques proudly displayed on his side credenza. Carl Johnson was a deliberately thoughtful leader and smart man with a masters in engineering from MIT. He became the president of Ocean Direct about seventeen years ago right after the previous president suddenly passed from a massive heart attack. Carl was the executive VP in charge of product development at the time but was always considered to be in the running as an incumbent when it was the right time. However, no one expected him to be made president since he had been with the company for only three years prior. In that short period of time, he had already established his worth to ODI and was promoted to the EVP role after only being onboard for less than a year, joining the company as senior manager of new product development. His ascension to the top spot came a lot sooner than anyone expected, but probably was just in the nick of time to save a floundering business operation that had not shown a profit to its corporate shareholders for the previous two years.

Upon taking the reins, he immediately closed the check book and had all purchases for goods and services channeled through office for final approval. This did not set well with the company controller, but this one act of leadership turned this company in the right direction within eighteen months, and the Board of Directors bestowed the title of CEO shortly thereafter.

I was hired a little after that to turn an unsupportive and apparently dysfunctional HR department around, as there were several incidences of employee malcontent and the threat of a union organizing attempt due to the general employee dissatisfaction and management apathy. This was always my strength and forte as I had experience with two other organizations as a change agent for positive employee relations which become an employer of choice in the community. Carl and I hit it off immediately as I recognized his sincere desire and goal to empower the entire organization to make Ocean Direct Inc. the best it could be in every area. He has been a tireless leader and positive role model for the senior management team by making his expectations very clear to all. He sets the tone and walks the talk even though the "old guard" management staffers still hang on to their ways, despite his leadership style.

Carl is very well-respected in the community for his contribution to various organizations designed to improve the quality of life for the underprivileged. I think it was my genuine work ethic and "can do" attitude that ingratiated me with Carl shortly after we met. I suspect many CEOs, top leaders in every organization, prefer a direct and frank answer to their questions as opposed to the usual BS and sugarcoated version they get way too often from their direct reports, in an attempt to placate the boss or minimize concern. That's the way I want my staff to communicate with me even when they have bad news or information they don't believe I will be happy to hear. I know Carl expects this from his direct reports and will only get honest and direct information from me.

"Okay, Bill, what is this all about with Alice?" Carl asks as he looks up from his downward gaze.

"Well, Carl, clearly we have some major push back on the decision to promote Alice into the assistant warehouse director position. If you recall, we discussed that this was going to be a distinct possibility when the decision was made. I'm not exactly sure where it's coming from just yet, but I have my suspicions. We'll get to the bottom of it as soon as we can, sir. I have Sarah involved, but I will be with her every step of the way."

Carl pauses for a few seconds, gives me a serious look, and then says, "I know you will make this a priority, Bill, and the sooner the better we get this resolved. We can't let this develop into an issue that causes any further disruptions among the warehouse team. You know my concern about Milken's commitment to move Alice into that role. We know it was the right thing to do for our company, and he better be behind it 100 percent, or I will need to address this sooner than later. We cannot afford to have any problem in that warehouse with the new business we're expecting. I've asked Sam to make that crystal to John, otherwise, we're going to need a backup plan, and you know what I mean. We all know Alice was far from ready to step into to that job, but we needed to make the move under the circumstances. And it's good to know Sarah is involved, she brings a lot of credibility to this matter, being a female, right?"

"Yes, Carl, I know you're concerned about John and his support, but for the moment, I don't sense he is being totally unsupportive. However, this matter is on the top of our list for resolution," I assured him.

"Good, I've got other fish to fry right now, Bill, and so you know this Wednesday I am out of the office for the balance of the week. How about we touch base next Monday, and you give me an update on this situation?" he says as he rises from his seat and escorts me to the door.

"Yes, sir, I'll have Jayne put me on your calendar for next Monday."

As I walk out of his office, I notice Jayne is tied up with three other people as I pass by her desk. I will reach out to her later on.

Walking back to my office, I am clearly aware of Carl's concern with this issue possibly becoming a major disruption for our warehouse as we ramp up operations with the new business orders. Carl has repeatedly stated to me that he will absolutely not tolerate the "good ol' boy" network operating out there any longer. In addition, it was Carl who went out on a limb supporting Alice for that role. He is not the type of leader who accepts failure very well. Accordingly, this is precisely why I assigned Sarah to be a regular presence out there to quickly pick up any dissention among the troops with the promotion of Alice in the new role. I had a strong feeling it would be some time before Alice would be fully accepted, but it has been six months, and for there to continue to be an issue, it has to end soon. Based on this latest incident, I'm now wondering if I have done enough to stay on top of it. This will require some careful planning and deliberate action from our department going forward. But just exactly what that will entail…not sure at this very moment, but I have made a commitment to my boss, and I intend to follow through.

I glance at the clock on the wall as I enter the HR office. Ten a.m., just in time for our Monday morning department staff meeting. I walk into the HR conference room where Sarah is presiding over the meeting so I slip into an open chair at the table.

"Good morning, folks," announcing my arrival. "Please, carry on, Sarah."

This is our weekly Monday meeting where we communicate ongoing matters of interest to the entire HR team. Each team member has ten minutes to share what they are currently working on, give updates to previous discussions, and bring up questions about any subject matter. I've encouraged all of them to be open, frank, and clear—nothing is off the table. This is their opportunity to speak their minds, inform each other of issues and matters of importance relevant to HR department operations. It has been a very good forum for clear and concise communication among the staff. This is their meeting; I am only there to learn what they are dealing with in their respective jobs and to answer any questions they may have. Separately, I hold a monthly staff meeting with my direct reports to discuss matters that I need to convey, and I regularly meet with each one of them individually on a weekly basis. Of course, I am always available any other time they need to speak with me…and that seems to be sufficient. I want them to always feel like no matter what their issue is, it is important to me. Human resources work does not follow the clock nor does it wait for us to be available. People have problems, concerns, and issues all the time and where we have a twenty-four-hour, seven-days-a-week operation, it can happen any time. To be a supportive and a responsive function, we have to be available always. How can I be any different with them?

Following the department meeting, I asked Sarah to give me an update on her discussions with Alice. We step into my office and close the door. Sarah informed me that she had contacted our IT department to pull the voice mails from Alice's desk phone, but they are telling her that these calls came from outside the company. They will need to get with the phone company to see if they can assist in determining where the calls originated from. Sarah asks if we should notify law enforcement should we need an approval for a trace of some kind. I told her to hold off on that right now; let's see what the phone company can tell us and we'll go from there. I was reluctant to bring law enforcement into this matter right now as it just seemed to be unnecessary. Instinctively, I wondered if I was intentionally minimizing the threat out of wishful thinking on my part or not wanting to heighten the matter to minimize undue concerns. In my opinion, we just didn't have enough to make that call right now.

At that moment, Sarah says, "Mr. McCallister, we have another issue I need to bring to your attention."

Oh boy, I'm thinking…what else are we going to have to deal with this morning, but of course, it is Monday! My mind is already anticipating the worst. My sarcasm isn't lost on Sarah as I give her that look of "what?".

"I know it's not the best time to drop this one on you, with everything going on with Alice, but I thought you would want to know," she says with reluctance.

"Just spit it out, Sarah," I blurted. "I already have a feeling that this is going to be the mother of all Mondays." Little did I really know how much that feeling would turn out to be prophetic.

"Well, you recall the drug ring we learned about operating out in the warehouse last year and those twelve employees who were connected?" Sarah starts.

"Yes, I certainly do. How could I forget about that so soon?" I said with complete dread with what I anticipate is coming next.

"Well…I believe we may still have an issue with drug dealing going on out there. Last night, Alphonso, the second shift supervisor, found several bags of powder which appear to be cocaine and amphetamine in baggies stuffed behind some cleaning supplies in a cabinet on the southside of the warehouse, just like exactly what was found on those guys who were busted out there last year," Sarah remarked.

"Okay, how much and any idea how it got there?" I asked instinctively.

"No, we're checking the cameras and hoping to identify who might've put it there," Sarah replied, continuing with, "it looks like the cocaine was divided up into several small bags as if they were ready to be distributed, and the amphetamine was all in one container, more than a hundred grey pills in count."

"Well, ain't that just marvelous," I quipped. "I wonder if this could be someone we missed from the gang that was operating right under our noses? Okay, keep me posted, Sarah. I'll need to inform Carl, and he'll want to know details. Thank you."

"Will do, sir," Sarah responded as she headed for the door.

"Oh, and Sarah…recheck the backgrounds on anyone hired or transferred into the warehouse within the last year, just in case this is a new person. Maybe we'll get lucky." I knew I was drawing straws with that statement, but you never know.

"Yes, of course, sir," Sarah said as she closed my door.

I clearly remember the incident with the drug ring we had operating out in the warehouse last year. The dirty dozen, as they were labeled when it all came out, had been selling drugs not only to our own employees but the general public as well…right under John Milken and his supervisor's noses! The only way this became discovered was because an inquisitive security guard noticed the frequent coming and goings of a former employee. He reported his observations to Sarah after notifying John and being told that this person was okay, just a good guy coming by to see old friends. However, the security guard thought it was odd that his visits were so frequent and was alerted when an employee reported a package in the men's room after video showed this former employee was last to enter and leave that area. The former employee would claim he was only stopping by the premises to see his friends but would later admit after being exposed by an undercover sting operation that he was delivering the goods to and collecting money from the dirty dozen team members who were distributing the product. The gang's primary business operation was away from the workplace, but occasionally, they sold on the premises; and by distributing to dealers within our warehouse, the ring could maintain anonymity from any outside police organization trying to track and identify the source of the drugs on the street as they would never suspect this activity coming from inside a reputable employer in the community. As what in many cases, someone gets greedy and decides they want to make more by taking an unusual chance, and this is how the sting worked to perfection. It was a great help that Sarah's brother worked in the narcotics division with the State Department of Law Enforcement. She was able to get an undercover officer secretly hired into the warehouse who was able to infiltrate the gang. In John's defense, if there is such a thing…a defense! His only mistake, a huge one, was allowing this former employee access to the premises unchallenged and those dealing the merchandise without suspecting there might be something suspicious about the number of times he dropped by on a regular basis. I guess three times a week for several months might be enough to alert most people; however, John and his management staff just thought he was a good guy who just missed his friends. Besides, he had done a credible job for us when he was employed here, and he was a former Marine. I'm not making any distinction that being a Marine should be a cause for concern, and in most cases, it is not a problem whatsoever. Anyone who makes that decision to serve their country by risking your life and may make the ultimate sacrifice is an honor beyond all in my book.

For the record, Mark Feinstein, my close friend, and his wife, Debbie, with whom CeCe and I spend most weekends within our group of five served in the marines as a jet pilot when he graduated from college. Both Charlie and I thought he was crazy and wondered if he had made a huge mistake. Not ever being in the service myself, nonetheless, I was always interested in hearing Mark tell stories about his adventures as a Marine vicariously. Since John was a former Marine, he obviously felt a strong kinship to Josh. Something

Mark would express when he related his Marine experiences, so I understand the special relationship those who serve as a Marine have. John and Josh had formed a close bond while he had worked for the company for five years before quitting to take another job. Just like many, we all overheard them discussing different events they had both endured while serving for our country. You could tell there was a primal connection between the two from their time in the Marines, even though it had clearly changed from John's era and Josh's.

Women? In the Marines? Ridiculous, what in the hell has happened to the honor and tradition of the greatest fighting force ever amassed in history? I can hear John bellowing this statement in my head. It was something John never could wrap his mind around, and Josh fed right into John's phobia with his own stories and examples of why women were just not made for the rigors and requirements of being a Marine. In retrospect, Josh took full advantage of his connection with John, and he played John like a fiddle when it came to trust. Obviously, we had rules on outsiders, former employees notwithstanding, gaining access to company premises. But John had his own rules, and he marches to his own drumbeat, to say the least. This entire incident became just another learning experience for our management team; we must enforce the written policy when it comes to allowing anyone not currently employed with ODI unfettered access to the premises, but then again, surely most reasonable would question why a former employee would continue to drop by, unannounced and so often, even if you thought highly of that individual. Now, it was a mandate from the CEO that every manager in the company was required to sign a document certifying that he/she understood and would strictly adhere to this policy. Completely unnecessary in my opinion, since we already had the policy in writing which everyone in the company was bound to follow. However, it definitely brought the matter to light, and I suppose it was necessary when you have those who require constant reminders to follow the written rules. Is it Friday yet? Hell no…I still have the rest of today and four more yet to go. God help me if the remainder of the week continues this way. It will be a long week, a very long week indeed!

The rest of the day goes fairly well, we do not have any other major pressing issues other than a few disgruntled team members who weren't pleased that their annual wage increases were not what they expected. This is an ongoing concern that comes to the HR department frequently because, evidently, some employees don't feel like they were given a fair performance evaluation and then when it is reflected in their pay, they don't seem to understand the correlation. You know, I've always wondered why an employee who legitimately feels this way doesn't want to seek clarity from the manager who delivered the evaluation. It just seems to me that if they asked the manager what they could do to improve then they would know how to get a bigger pay increase next time. This lack of dynamic interaction or "avoidance" between the manager and direct report when it comes to performance evaluations has always perplexed me. However, it seems like they would rather have a third party get involved to get an answer. It's that potential confrontational conversation that makes people uneasy—nobody wants to have it—but it really doesn't have to be that way at all. Employees need to know where they stand; generally, they want to know how they're doing on the job. But invariably, managers sometimes avoid giving direct feedback on job performance for fear of demoralizing or deflating the employee. This seems to be a common problem in most work places as well. I hear this from my other HR colleagues frequently. It's like "pulling teeth" to get managers to do timely performance reviews, and HR people struggle to understand why it has to be this way at all.

When I arrive home at 6:45, I walk through the kitchen door from the garage, toss my briefcase on the table, and contemplate whether I should go straight for the bourbon. Instead, I settle for a glass of cold water from the fridge; it's still a bit early. Besides, I consciously avoid drinking when stressed. Just driving home with the evening commuters can be unnerving by itself absent any aggravation from the day. I hear a vaguely audible but familiar sound from the direction of CeCe's office followed by some unintelligible conversation which tells me she's talking with a client, no doubt. I walk into her office area—a converted third bedroom—we nod together in unison, and I kiss her softly on the forehead. As she returns to her conversation, I exit her domain and head to our bedroom to get into more comfortable clothes, usually a pair of shorts and t-shirt. I like to be comfortable when I am at home...who doesn't? I work my way into the great room, turn on the TV to catch the last few minutes of the news, and settle into my comfy and well-worn recliner. One of these days I'm going to get a new chair, I definitely need a new one for sure. But I haven't found another one that I like so far, but I haven't seriously been looking either.

Not long enough after the news finishes, my wife comes into the room and plops down on my lap as I am fully reclined back, about to close my eyes, quickly heading for a quick cat nap.

"How was your day, sweetie?" she asks, not really seeking response. Because before I could get a word out, she blurts, "Guess what?"

Of course, that is the universal signal to give the genuine look of interest, so of course I do.

"I just landed a big assignment with First Commercial to head up development plans for their new location going up over on Fifth Street next to the Cadillac dealership!"

"Oh, really? Great, that's awesome honey!" I respond with exaggerated enthusiasm.

"Keep it up, you," she quips. "Bill, this is a really big deal for us. It could be a six-figure job, oh ye of little faith."

"I'm sorry, babe…just funning with you. I'm really happy you got this assignment. I know it means a lot," I say as I pull her face close and kiss her lips.

"Hey, let's celebrate tonight, you up for that?" she squeals.

You bet I know the right answer here. "Absolutely!" I say without any hesitation, even though my plans were to relax in my chair, and I am actually beginning to question my earlier decision not have that bourbon.

"I'll get a reservation for us at Ruth Chris. Eight o'clock okay?"

"Okay, Bill. But I don't think we need reservations for tonight, darling—it's Monday," as she pops up and runs off to the bedroom.

Of course, she's right; what was I thinking? A reservation just seemed like the right thing to say whenever a celebration of any kind is in order. I slowly get up from my comfortable chair and head to get a quick shower and change into some different attire. Somehow, shorts and a t-shirt just won't go with the event.

For the rest of the night, we toasted her new assignment enjoying a nice meal and sharing a bottle of their best Cabernet. Cecelia is not one to be overly extravagant when it came to celebrating big events in life. She always held to the belief that we should celebrate living every day and be thankful for the good times, but not to the point of overindulgence. She was a firm believer that if you over-celebrated the good times then the tough times will be more difficult; kind of like keeping things on an even keel, you might say. Just another reason I continue to be strongly attracted to this woman after all these years. She keeps me balanced even when I don't realize she's doing it.

While enjoying the meal and celebrating CeCe's good news, I ask if she had heard anything from the girls about Charlie from the weekend. She gives me that, "Really?" look and then says, "Oh, Bill. Let's not talk about Charlie tonight, okay?"

All righty then, I know when it's time to switch the subject, so I quickly segue into asking about the upcoming weekend, even though it's only Monday evening.

"So, anything planned for this weekend with the group?"

She shakes her head slowly from side to side and then gives me that other look, the one that tells me she has "other" things on her mind. *Okey dokey*, I thought as I quickly gulp the last of my Cabernet.

"Waiter, check please." I clear my throat and motion by signing my name in the air. We left the restaurant arm in arm.

About ten minutes later, heading home, both of us anxious to explore our natural instincts with the mellowness of wine in our heads. Untypical for us; for the most part, we satisfy our sexual urges on the weekends when we are both more relaxed. But this will also be a great evening for sure. Now, we are not the most sexually active couple at this point in our lives, but when CeCe is "in the mood," as they say, that can turn me into a voracious tiger in the bedroom. Of course, as a typical male I'm already waiting for her on the bed with nothing but the sheet covering me from waist down as she exits the bathroom. When I tell you there is absolutely nothing more beautiful to me than seeing CeCe standing in the bathroom doorway with light accentuating the outline of her body through her negligee, I am telling you it is not with any influence of wine. I almost lose it as she slowly makes her way over to me. *Thank you, Lord, for this woman*, I almost hear myself saying. Needless to say, she has and continues to turn me on even if the years and having two children have changed her proportions to some degree. Nonetheless, she has continued to keep herself in good shape, and for a woman in her sixties, she is still a sight to see, and let me tell you, she is all woman when she is turned on! That innate animal instinct we all have in us, let me just say, CeCe hasn't lost anything over the years. As for me…I am the typical male animal when it comes to my wife as she can change my mood with just a look. Of course, all she has to do is provide a mental suggestion, and I am putty in her hands. Yes, indeed, this Monday has turned into one of the better ones, that's for sure!

The next morning, I awake with a suddenness that I don't usually experience when the 6:00 a.m. alarm goes off. Most times, I have the impression of a faraway buzzing sound that keeps getting louder and louder until I recognize it for what it is. That damn alarm clock! But today, I am shocked into sitting bolt upright in bed, which strikes me as very strange. What the hell am I so jumpy about? Could this be a premonition of things to come? Was last night just too damn relaxing to my senses that the alarm clock has shocked me back into my normal reality? It feels very strange, for sure.

Don't get me wrong; I've always enjoyed my job, but dealing with disturbed people and their issues for as long as I've been at it is quite taxing to you, not only mentally, but I'm sure there's a long-term physical component as well. I'll probably learn all about that after I've retired for ten years, and some psychoanalysts in the future will determine that old HR leaders have some negative residual effects from the job they had for so many years that they're just now discovering. I do know that in the short-term, it does affect your ability to always be on top of your game if you know what I mean? I think most men over forty understand exactly what I'm referring to. I'm just sayin'! Last night was *not* one of those times; making love with CeCe was as good as it gets for me and maybe as good as it's been in a very long time. She was so responsive and eager; it just fired up that animal instinct in me, and I wanted it to go on forever. Well, ah…er, let's just say we were engaged in each other for quite a while. It was after 1:00 p.m. by the time I set up the sleep interrupter for 6:00 a.m.

I glance over at CeCe, and she hasn't moved a muscle even with my wild thrashing, an uncharacteristic response to the alarm clock. I reach over to gently rub her hair, one of my favorite rituals whenever we are being affectionate and something we don't do nearly as often as we used to. I hear a faint moan of appreciation, but I know from past experience she is not ready to face the morning reality yet, so I turn and slip out of bed, still wondering why I was so alarmed by the alarm clock this morning. Something just doesn't compute in my head right now. Maybe it was finishing off the rest of the bottle of cab we enjoyed last night. Now, that isn't my usual routine for a weekday night, so it's possible my senses were just on alert when the alarm rang. I head to the bathroom and begin my daily ritual in preparation for that long drive into the office. "Another day, another dollar," I recall my parents bemoaning the start of the workday when I was a kid, and it's only Tuesday, still a long time until Friday…will I make it? We'll see, but the day is just getting started, and I have a lot on my plate today.

As I travel down the interstate toward the office, the traffic is typical for 8:00 a.m. on a Tuesday, packed and dangerous. There must be a dozen of wrecks every week on the highways in the morning leading into the city. Most commuters are still trying to wake up, some are gulping coffee like it's going out of style, and then there are the idiot hot-rod-late-to-work drivers weaving in and out of lanes, trying to break existing land speed records. Did I mention how dangerous driving into work has become in the morning? Just then, my cell phone goes off, and I can tell it's an incoming office call, "Good morning, this is Bill McCallister."

A voice on the other end screams, "Mr. McAllister, this is Tim. We have a problem here at the warehouse. There was an assault on one of our employees from a group of men who came in through the employee's entrance, these people had weapons and masks and had everyone lie down on the floor. Sir, they tied everyone's hands behind their back with zip ties. They grabbed Rafael Rodriquez and took him outside," Tim was still screaming into the phone.

"Hold on, Tim," I say loudly, trying to get a word in between his animated rants. I decided it might be safer if I pulled over to the shoulder of the road; this was not what I expected to hear on my way to work! Tim Jernigan is a warehouse supervisor who has worked for us for several years. He had a special allegiance to the HR Department going back a few years when John Milken wanted to fire him for insubordination, and we stepped into the breach on his behalf and threw up the stop sign. A classic case of Milken overstepping his authority to fire someone without a proper investigation. Tim was one of the few warehouse supervisors who refused to be a "yes" man for Milken's way.

Milken made a veiled comment in a management meeting accusing HR of protecting some employees who were not loyal to W/H management. Carl had shut him down as it was not the place for that discussion, but that was typical for John. He had made his point; there was no further discussion. "Has anyone been hurt?" I interrupt Tim in mid-sentence.

"Well, Rafael was beaten up pretty bad and left in the parking lot, but I think he's going to be okay. He doesn't want to go to the hospital, his face is cut, and he's bleeding, but we were able to get the bleeding to stop," Tim responds.

"Where is the security guard right now, Tim?" I ask.

"He's in the security shack pulling surveillance from the cameras. They've already called the police, guess they will be here sometime soon," Tim responds.

"Okay, son, thanks for the call, I'll be getting there in a little while. Has someone called John Milken and let him know what's happened?" I ask, expecting Tim to say he would rather that I do that.

"Yes, sir, he was my first call," Tim responds.

"Good man, see you soon," I click off the phone, a bit surprised by his answer, knowing the ongoing tension between them over John's attempt to send him packing a few years ago.

Well, there you go. Great, another issue coming from that warehouse. It seems like it just keeps getting better now, every day! We all understand and realize that the warehouse is our "bread and butter," as they say. Without it, we are not in business, and despite the constant challenges generated out there, we remain a very profitable company. However, I often wonder how much longer the board and CEO are going to continue to allow Milken to run that place. That operation could be the shining star of Ocean Direct; instead, everyone has to mollycoddle the W/H director as he continues to fumble his way through mismanaging his staff with his old-school antics and lack of commitment to basic human decency. While John may not have had anything directly to do with this latest episode, no one can doubt his lack of proper management and care for his employees out there has to be a contributing factor. It's a "Cluster f——k," as they say in the military, and I've never served, even I know that.

Okay, so my drive into the office this morning has now made the day take on an entirely new direction. So masked men burst into the warehouse this morning, tied everyone up but target one, a certain employee, and took him out into the parking lot, roughed him up, and then left. And then he refuses medical treatment? Hmm, no doubt this could be related to the internal drug ring we had operating out in the warehouse last year and the small bags of cocaine recently discovered in a warehouse cleaning storage cabinet. Great, we still have drugs and gangs operating within our walls! So this will consume a huge part of my day now, just when I thought I might be able to get ahead of my schedule. Thank God I have great staff who knows how to pick up the slack when these unexpected detours happen in our world of employee-problem resolution. Without having them, I'm sure I would've taken early retirement or gotten fired for incompetence or maybe just ended it all myself, wait, what? I can't even begin to think like that. Getting to the end now is my one and only primary goal!

After arriving at the office and getting the specific details of the assault on our employee Rafael and the unnecessary terror inflicted on the other employees, thankfully, there were only three other early arrivals with Rafael that were subjected to this ordeal as they entered the building this morning. Sarah and her crew spent most of the morning consoling the three women who were tied up and scared half out of their wits by these thugs. We gave them the rest of the week off with pay and referred them to meet with our outside employee-assistance program contact and their professional counseling team to help them overcome the shock of this event. All three mentioned that they sincerely appreciated the company's kind offer, but they would be okay and pass on the counseling. I got the feeling that all of them had experienced much worse incidents in their lives and that being given the rest of the week off with pay was more important.

Of course, John Milken had to throw his two cents worth into that decision.

"What the hell?" he questions.

"They were just tied up, nobody got hurt, except the dirtbag they came here for, and he probably owed 'em money and deserved it. Why are we paying these three for the rest of the week off? Ridiculous!" He explodes behind closed doors when we tell him the plan.

This was classic John in all his glory, a perfect example of supreme lack of care and compassion for his own employees. Obviously, Rafael was the prime target of the attack, which was clearly sent as a message directly to him, despite no admission of knowing any of the perpetrators. Of course, Milken is convinced Rafael is involved in the finding of coke on the premises based on this event and the continual evidence of drug activity right under his nose. When the police arrived, they questioned Rafael for two hours, and without getting much information from him, they reviewed the security tapes and then collected what little evidence there was.

At least they were frank and up-front by explaining there was almost no chance of apprehending anyone for this event. However, only after I expressed my disappointment did they agree to step up patrols in the area more often for the next few weeks in case these three hoodlums decide to show up again. As I said, there is no hope anyone will be held accountable for the attack, but what's even more incriminating, Rafael didn't seem to be pushing for justice at all, but this was not a complete surprise at this point. When I met with Carl later in the day and mentioned Milken's response to the whole affair, he was not surprised even one little bit.

So I go ahead and come right out and ask Carl, "When are we going to realize that John Milken is just not the right person to be running the most important operation in our company?"

"Well, Bill, you know the answer to that, and frankly, I'm surprised you're even asking me that question. You, of all people, know we don't have anyone else who is remotely capable of keeping a lid on that place right now. With your insistence that we promote Alice into the assistant warehouse director position, we are stuck with John until we have someone else capable," Carl snaps.

"So John is it for now. Look, Bill, I don't like it any more than you do, but we don't have another option," he continues.

One thing for sure, I know when to shut up when it comes to debating Carl, especially when his mind is made up. But he could not be any more accurate; we don't have any other choice, and John Milken knows that too.

Well, it gets even better; the local television station got wind of the event from who and how, but we'll never know the answer to that question. This is the small regional television station that covers the events and news for the tri-county area. Typically, they cover mostly local human-interest stories and, of course, report on national events they pick up from the AP wires and major news outlets. But when there's a local crime event or public safety issue, all of a sudden, they're the self-appointed protector of the community, and a story like this can be stretched out for several days, especially if there's little hope of anyone being held responsible. It's like a perfect scenario for them to jump on and show the concerned citizens and viewers that they are on top of something that could be of interest, especially if it involves drugs, sex, or harm to a member of the community, kind of like sensationalistic journalism. Okay, I need to wind it back somewhere. I know they're just doing their jobs. I just don't understand why everything has to be made such a big deal, especially if it has to do with negativity. I think I'm answering my own question!

So, of course, at 3:00 p.m., I got a call from the receptionist that there was a reporter from the TV station in the lobby to talk with someone from the company in response to the event early this morning. Since Carl does not enjoy being in front of the media, and he shuns the idea of sharing any information about the company with the public, I was nominated to meet with the TV reporter waiting in our front lobby with a camera crew. As I made my way out to the lobby, I was going over in my head what I should say on this matter. I didn't think there would be anything specific that would make this incident newsworthy to anyone outside of ODI other than we would be pursuing everything possible to eliminate this from happening again and that we're working with local law enforcement. Yes, this would be a safe and responsible statement to the media; while not unexpected, it would be the correct thing to do at this time. Maybe so extremely mundane and uninteresting that the locals might decide that it was not even worthy to air on the six o'clock news.

As I approached the outer lobby, I could see the television representative and was surprised that the person standing there was not just one of their field reporters but their evening anchor personality, Beth Spenser. Now, this woman has been a staple for Channel 54 for the past ten years and reported on many of the biggest stories that have crossed their news desk. In her earlier years, she was known as "Bulldog Beth" for relentless digging into the detail of those she interviewed to get information.

I open the door and greet her, "Hi, Beth, I'm Bill McCallister, HR director for Ocean Direct. How are you, and how can I help you?"

"Oh, you recognize me then, ah, Mr. McCallister, is it?" she says, extending her hand.

"Yes, but please call me Bill," I respond.

"Sure, Bill, nice to meet you," she says as she looks down to write in her notes. "As you may surmise, I'm here to get a statement from Ocean Direct on the event that occurred earlier this morning, thank you for cooperating. Now, to get us started, I will ask you to tell us what you know about the incident and any other information you might have about why this occurred. But first, before I start, let's move you over here in front of this wall there for better lighting" She gently places her hand on my shoulder and guides me to the right. "Do you have any questions?" she speaks quickly and purposely, obviously in an attempt to eliminate any objections to her directions.

Noticing the cameraman was getting into position, "Beth, will this be live or taped for later showing?" I ask.

"This is being recorded for either the six o'clock or ten thirty broadcast, Bill," she responds. "Okay, if you don't have any more questions, let's go ahead with the interview, five, four, three, two, one, go! I'm now standing in front of the large mural depicting a fleet of fishing vessels."

Before I could even ask anything further, she signals her camera operator, and with that, this extremely bright blinding light is shown directly into my eyes, and she begins her bit, "Good evening, I'm Beth Spencer Channel 54, and I'm here with Bill McCallister, a company representative to learn more about the horrible event that occurred last night here on the premises of Ocean Direct. Now, Mr. McCallister, police officers responded to a call around 5:45 this morning involving the report of a group of masked men who came on your premises unexpectedly brandishing weapons and forcefully dragging an employee from the warehouse building. They then beat him in the parking lot, and as we understand it, this all happened in front of several other employees who were also pushed around, terrorized, and tied up as well. There was an anonymous report that perhaps this could have been related to drug activity on the premises, and we'd like to confirm this if possible. We're there any other casualties from the incident?" she says without pausing for a breath and pushing a microphone into my face.

"Uh, well, we're still investigating the incident," I stammer as I was thinking about how to phrase my next statement.

"Okay, I understand," she interrupts, "no problem, but can you tell our viewers if this incident could be related to any possible drug activity?"

"Well, with all due respect," I say firmly, "I'm not aware of any specific drug activity at this point, and I'm not sure how much more detail I can give you as this matter is still under police investigation, and other than the basic information you mentioned, we don't have anything else to report at this time."

"Okay, Mr. McAllister," she responds, "can Ocean Direct provide a statement and any possible explanation of why this event occurred on your property this morning and why a specific person was targeted? It seems quite unusual to have masked intruders come into a place of business and attack a specific individual unless there is something else related to the matter. As a responsible voice in the community WEDC, Channel 54 would like to assure the general public that they should have no concern about their own safety and welfare."

At that very moment, it occurred to me that she was implying that Ocean Direct might be under investigation for drug activity on the premises. Obviously, this was coming from the police department and was mentioned to the TV station. This explains why they sent one of their big guns down here to put ODI on the spot regarding this accusation.

"Well, first, let me say that we have absolutely no idea what caused this unacceptable action by those responsible, and going forward, we are taking every precaution possible to protect our employees from anything like this ever happening again on our premises. And second, as mentioned, the matter is being investigated by the police, and we will be interested to learn what they find out and such, will pursue every option available to prosecute those responsible. In the meantime, we will be adding additional security to prevent any other future outside intrusion into our facility. We are a large employer in the area and, unfortunately, a target for undesirables who decide there may be something to gain by this action. We will not tolerate that happening here and will continue to cooperate with law enforcement to protect our employees and the general public," I state, staring directly into the camera.

"Well, okay then," Beth says in her most professional voice, turning to face the camera, "There you have it, you heard directly from an executive of the company. The company is cooperating with the local police on this matter to bring those responsible for this criminal activity to justice, so stay tuned for any further developments. This is Beth Spencer from the lobby of Ocean Direct, Channel 54 News Team, your local news, happening every day, all the time."

After exchanging parting pleasantries with Ms. Spencer, I reiterated to her that obviously, ODI does not condone the activity that occurred this morning as we will support local police efforts to get to the bottom of the matter soon.

The rest of my day was typical, one that passed without any further issues, but I couldn't help but wonder why the police decided it was appropriate to mention to the TV station that the incident this morning may have been related to drug activity when that wasn't even discussed with us. Everybody seems to have opinions, but very few have solutions. Welcome to my world!

On my drive home that day, I tried to keep my thoughts in perspective and not focus on John Milken and his ridiculous ranting. I couldn't help but wonder why we have so many different and such diverse opinions in this country about how we should help those who face hardships and challenges in life. Take our own elected officials who can't seem to agree on much of anything. Clearly, it seems like the predominant political party in the US. Republicans and Democrats constantly oppose every idea the other presents all the time. Why is that? We elect representatives to city, county, state, and national offices to do the people's business. However, all that seems to ever happen is a constant effort of disagreement on how things should operate, how tax dollars are spent, and who gets credit for what. Is this really what our founding forefathers envisioned as a productive working society for the betterment of the people?

Take my close friends Charlie and Mark. You couldn't ask for two better friends to have. So what if Charlie may partake of his favorite spirits more than he should on occasion; okay, *often* is the operative word here. These guys are really good people even though they both married above their pay grades, and they would give me the shit off their backs if I needed it. But as far as politics, they could not be farther apart on how they believe a government should be operated. Charlie is a die-hard conservative and makes no bones about whenever the subject comes up. Of course, Mark, coming from a Jewish faith, leans heavily to the liberal democratic side.

You can imagine the debates that rage when these two get a little "hooch" in 'em and start arguing the politics of the day. Many times, I had to step in and separate these two so-called good friends just before they started throwing punches literally. Charlie doesn't believe the government should give a dime of collected tax dollars to anyone who can work and any country that doesn't fully support the principles by which the United States operates. Mark is defiantly opposed to closed borders and anti-social programs that benefit only the wealthy. And when the subjects of state's rights, abortion, and gun control come up, well, that's usually when the party is doomed to be over real soon.

There is simply no compromise with either one of these two on these issues, and their arguments can quickly become nasty, name-calling, mudslinging episodes quickly, which makes almost no one happy to witness. During the year leading up to the last presidential election, Charlie being the consummate "Keep America Great" fanatical supporter and Mark trashing Trump at every opportunity, you can imagine the "knockdown, drag-out" debates (if you want to call them that!) we were subjected to. I was never so happy when election day was here, and the anticipation of an end of the heightened arguments over who would win the White House would be settled. However, saying I was ever so disappointed in these two friends would be the understatement of the year.

Instead of calming things down, much like what has happened in our country, nothing changed between these two close friends, and if anything, they debate even more about the future political process and what will change when their party gets or keeps control. The reality of the matter is that *nothing ever changes*! The rhetoric doesn't change, no matter who wins and who loses, it gets even worse. I think the losers in elections become even more emboldened as they have the opportunity to blame what happens next on the current administration.

The unfortunate part of all this is that I believe most Americans (black, white, Hispanic, Asian, and others) do not fully support any political party over another but have different opinions based on the specific subject being considered. But God forbid if you are a Republican and you aren't in favor of reversing Roe V. Wade, or if you are a Democrat and you do not support gun control. These could be blasphemous opinions in the eyes of the political party you identify with. I truly believe most Americans would prefer that elected officials should serve the better good of all whom they represent, not just those who are major contributors and special interest groups. Clearly, our political system is broken today, and nothing appears to be any way to fix it, especially since there are such hardline beliefs between the two prevailing political parties in this country. We all lose when there is absolutely no compromise or unification of effort. That's my two cents, and I approve of this message! Well, it is comical, to say the least. Just consider what has taken place in the last ten years or so; it has really been a circus, and that's putting it kindly!

After arriving home and walking in the door, CeCe yells from her office, "Hey you! I saw you on TV at 6:00. You looked delicious! But I'm jealous of that Beth Spencer, she has no right standing so close to *my* man like that! I bet she got a good whiff of that awesome-smelling cologne you wear. I saw the way she was eyeballing you!"

I walk into her office and ask, "So they aired the interview already?"

"Oh yeah," CeCe says, "and based on how it was reported, I guess there's a serious drug problem in John Milken's warehouse. Bill, when are you and Carl going to get rid of that guy? You know this is only going to get worse as time goes on, right?"

"*What?* What are you talking about?" I ask. "There was nothing said in the interview about a drug problem at ODI, where did that come from?" I say irritatingly.

"Okay, honey, I'm just saying how the news report went, don't be upset at me," CeCe snaps back. "The report started out that there was confirmed drug activity going on out in the ODI warehouse, and even though the company has not admittedly it, top management was adamant about working with the police to bring those responsible to justice, and then your interview was shown with that haughty Beth Spencer. I don't like her, Bill. She was deliberately trying to bait you into admitting that drug activity had something to with the incident this morning, and anybody with a brain could tell that, but I think you handled the interview very well." She smiles, looking back over her shoulder.

"Oh boy," I sigh. "What a mess this has all become? I can't believe Carl hasn't called me yet." Just then, my cell phone rang. "Hi, Carl, guess you calling about the TV report?" I anticipate his reaction.

"Bill, I don't want you to worry, but I need you to listen, we've received word of a threat made against your life. There is an off-duty police officer on his way to your home shortly to be sure you and Cecelia are kept safe tonight. He will stay there through tomorrow until the threat can be legitimized," Carl says very solemnly.

"Carl, what? What do you mean by an off-duty police officer? What is going on, Carl?" My voice raises in obvious shock.

"Bill, listen to me, this is no joke, it's serious." Carl's voice is now audibly shaking. "I'm so sorry to have to tell you this, but as I mentioned, a police officer will be at your home soon to ensure you are safe until they check this threat out. We were informed a few minutes ago that a police informant had told police that you are being considered a target by a known Mexican drug cartel and that your life could be in danger. Obviously, this could be related to what's going on in the warehouse since you were involved in the television report this evening. Apparently, you are being targeted as the company representative at the center of this threat. Bill, I apologize for all this, but there is no option here. The DEA has relayed this information to the local police, and it's being checked out to find out if it is actually a real threat. They did say that many times these things do not actually turn out to be real, just false alarms among those who deal in these matters. They don't have any more information right now, but until they can get further confirmation, they wanted us to be aware of your safety. We should know more tomorrow, but this is just a precaution." Carl's voice is a little more stable but no less consoling as I'm not sure even he believes what he is saying.

"Carl, I don't know what to say, we're not aware of any specific drug trafficking activity in the warehouse, and if there are drugs out there, I don't have any information about who, what, where, or when. All we know for sure is that a few small bags of cocaine were found out there, so why would someone be targeting me or anyone else in the company for that?" I question.

"Bill, listen to me," Carl interrupts, "you are just the face of the company right now, this may be an overreaction from the hoodlums who busted in there this morning, and since you were on TV talking about justice for those that did this, possibly this could just be a scare tactic to get us to drop the matter, we just don't know anything specific right now, but we have to take precautions." Carl explains,

"Just plan on staying home tomorrow until we know more and you hear from me. I will call you as soon as I get an update from the police, but someone from the police department will be calling you soon and give you information about the off-duty officer who will be arriving at your home shortly."

"Okay, Carl, I don't know what else I can do but wait for more information, but please let me know as soon as you know what's going on," my voice filled with obvious concern.

"Absolutely, Bill, I'll call you as soon as I know anything," Carl reassures. "Just don't worry about this, I'm sorry to break this to you, but I thought you'd want to know before the officer showed up at your home."

As I click off my phone, I notice the sheer look of concern on CeCe's face as she gives me that look, begging for an immediate explanation. Before she can even say anything, I begin explaining everything Carl has revealed to me, but I downplay the part about the officer coming to the house to ensure my safety. I do not want her to worry about any of this, as who knows? Maybe this is just an over-reaction to my statements made in the TV interview, as Carl said. I certainly don't need CeCe to have any concerns right now, especially since I have more than enough concerns for the both of us.

Just then, my phone rings, and I look to see who it could be. Charlie, talk about bad timing; I don't really want to answer, but I know if I don't, he will just keep ringing me until I do. He never leaves a voice mail.

"Charlie, how's it going, buddy?" I say in my best fake voice.

"Billy boy, my main man, my TV star celebrity friend, how you doing? Got any Hollywood offers yet? I saw your TV interview with that hot Beth Spencer, is she a babe or what with those giant hooters!" Charlie's voice is animated.

"Charlie, yes, glad you caught the interview, but can I call you back in a bit?" I try to interrupt, "I'm sort of in the middle of something right now."

"Whoa, bud, what's up? Sorry to have bothered you, man, so you and the misses involved in some serious shit, huh?" he laughs, "I was hoping to drop by and go over details on the golf tournament we're playing in next week. I'll bring some of that nasty Four Roses crap you like, and we'll make our plans kick some ass."

"Uh, Charlie, seriously not a good time right now, I'll call you back in a little while," I cut him off, but knowing that's not easy, especially when he's had a few drinks, which is like, every day!

"Okay, man, I get it. You don't wanna talk to ol' Charlie right now, I understand. Call me later if you think I'm worth the effort," his voice expresses disgust and then hangs up abruptly.

Okay, I guess I'll need to make that up to him as I know he won't let go of it until I do.

CeCe begins asking about the call from Carl, and I'm trying hard to downplay the blatantly obvious concern I now have, but she knows me too well, which means she ain't buying.

"Okay, Bill," she starts. "Why would Carl be calling you at home now to talk about some nobody making an idle threat against the company for a TV interview you did, and as expected, to explain what happened in the warehouse this morning? That just makes absolutely no sense to me at all. So do you want to tell me exactly what's going on, or do you want me to just worry myself sick?" she asks. "And, by the way, why is Charlie talking to you about Beth Spencer's tits? Huh? Is this what you guys do? Go around looking at women's boobs, and then ya'll talk about 'em later over drinks? Come on, what is going on with all that, hmmm?" As she puts her face right up into mine.

"Uh, okay, well, you know I can't answer that without some self-incrimination!" I nervously respond.

But then I notice that her face has the biggest smile, so I smile back and look away, hoping I don't have to do any more explaining. But she asks again about the phone call with Carl, and I know she will be pestering me until I come clean. So I have her sit down with me on the couch, and I take her hand in mine. I clear my throat because the comment about Charlie talking about Beth Spencer's boobs has me a bit choked up. I go on to explain everything that Carl has told me. I went over all the details about the informant, the DEA, and a police officer that will be arriving to talk with us.

Surprisingly, CeCe does not freak out or fly off the handle about anything I have said. She just nods as I explain what I was told and gives me a look of concern but does not panic at all, which I did not expect at all. I really thought she might think the worst, but actually, I shouldn't have been surprised at all. Hell, I'm the one who seems to be more panicked about all this than anyone, even Carl. At least he was trying to reassure me that everything would be okay. As if I didn't know already, CeCe really is the rock in our relationship; without her, I am not half the person I am today. Just talking all this through with her makes me feel better about the whole thing, at least for now. But I can't help but think, *Could there be real danger about being too casual about this?* I guess we'll see what happens next; just then, my phone rings again, and it's a number I do not recognize. Should I answer or let the call go to voice mail? CeCe notices my initial hesitation, "Go ahead, Bill, it could be the police officer Carl told you would be calling." Yes, of course, she's right; she's always right as usual!

I answer the call, and the caller identifies himself as Lieutenant David Masters from the Metro Police Department, asking if we were okay and inform that Detective Dale Ingersoll would be arriving within the next half hour to introduce himself and let us know what he would be doing while the threat was being investigated. He will be here to keep watch while the information they received is being verified. In most cases, Lieutenant Masters assures me that these threats are usually baseless and on very few occasions have any one of them turned out to be legitimate. However, since this information was being conveyed from an inside informant, they wanted to be sure of its authenticity. Wait, what? Very few have turned out to be legitimate? So a few have been real? *That* didn't give me much comfort at all.

Anyway, I was given the details about what we should and should not do for the rest of the evening, and the detective would provide more detail when he arrived. In addition, more information would be forthcoming based on their investigation. Roughly thirty minutes later, there was a knock on our front door, and the doorbell rang. I looked out the window, and there stood a rather large imposing young man who looked like a college football player dressed in a blue suit. Clearly, he played ball for some college before becoming a cop; if not, there was a recruiter who has deep regrets, that was for sure.

I slowly open the door, and I hear a voice say, "Mr. McCallister, I'm Detective Ingersoll with the Metro Police Department, and I trust you've been expecting me?"

"Why, yes, yes, sir. I was told to ask for your identification," I say almost apologetically.

"Absolutely, sir." He holds up an ID card attached to a leather bifold with a gold badge with the words MPD across the top and *detective* on the bottom. I opened the door and directed him inside. We spent the next two hours going over what he was assigned to be doing for the night and into the morning. Basically, he would set up in our living room, occasionally stepping outside to check the perimeter of the house. We were told that we should not leave the house or even step outside from this point on. In addition, it would be best to keep all lights turned off and only use a flashlight for short periods of time if we needed to move about the house.

Okay, talk about a bit unsettling. This was downright scary stuff to hear for both of us. From that moment on, CeCe stayed attached to my left arm, and if not holding it tightly, she sure wasn't more than a few inches away at any time.

"Bill, we're going to get through this okay, right?" she asks after about an hour, waiting for darkness.

"Of course, darling," I assure her, "this is just precautionary. I don't believe they have any reason to worry at this point, but as the sergeant said, and the detective has confirmed, they'll know more by tomorrow. Let's just go lie down and see if we can get some sleep."

Surprisingly, I had this calmness come over me, and while CeCe has always been the one who has the serene demeanor between the two of us, her show of concern has given me confidence that I did not realize I had, at least for the moment.

Needless to say, neither CeCe nor I get much sleep. Between the two, I think one or both of us were awake during the entire night. From time to time, I was keenly aware of someone standing outside the bedroom window, and I got up a couple of times to investigate, and sure enough, I could make out Detective Ingersoll's silhouette in the dim light as he made his rounds outside the house.

When morning finally arrived, which seemed forever coming, I left CeCe sleeping and quietly slipped out of our bedroom to check in with the detective. As I rounded the hallway corner and entered the living room, I noticed the officer lying on the couch, facing the cushions with his back toward me. I gently called out his name to announce my presence. I did not see any visible movement, and there was no immediate response, so I took a few steps closer to the couch and spoke again to get his attention, but still no movement or acknowledgment of my presence. I did not want to startle him as I was thinking he might be sleeping. After all, staying up most of the night, the man must be exhausted.

The last thing I wanted to do was cause an overreaction in a way that might not be good for me. But after a couple of seconds, I started thinking something was not right here; he should've heard me by now. Now my mind was racing; has something happened to him? Is he okay? Was it possible that someone got inside last night? Could the person still be somewhere in the house? My mind instantly went to CeCe. Instinctively, I gently placed my hand on his shoulder, which was a big mistake! The figure lying on my couch suddenly turned, and in literally what was half a second, I was staring at the wrong end of an automatic handgun. Of course, my heart right went to my throat, and I felt weak in the knees, almost losing my balance, falling to the floor.

"Mr. McCallister, is everything okay?" the voice asks in a loud commanding tone.

"Oh God," I cry out, "you scared the living shit out of me. I'm so sorry to wake you, I…uh…I…ah."

"It's okay, sir, are you and your wife okay? Is anything wrong?" Detective Ingersoll asks as he lowers his gun from my face, and I am instantly relieved, to say the least.

All the loud voices and commotion brought CeCe out of the bedroom.

"Bill, Bill? Where are you? Is everything all right?" she screams as she runs down the hall, clutching her nightgown. "Oh my God, is something wrong?" she cries out.

"No, honey, no, everything is fine. I just startled the officer when I came out to check on things, but it's okay." I say with a deep sigh.

"Yes, we are fine, Mrs. McCallister," Detective Ingersoll assures her as he slides open the window drapes to peer out into the early morning light.

"Oh, thank God, Bill, we made it through the night," CeCe moans as she grabs my arm and then around the waist, helping me to my feet.

"Mr. McCallister, I'm going to step out and check the perimeter and make a few phone calls, I'll be back in just a few minutes," Ingersoll says as he slowly opens the front door.

I turn to CeCe who was still holding me tightly and kiss her forehead in great relief that, indeed, we have made it through the night. The question before us now was how would the day go? What would be in store for us today?

Well, the answer to that was "not much" for the rest of the morning. I received a call from Carl, checking in to see that we were okay and if we had heard anything further from the police. In addition to a call from Lieutenant Masters letting us know that the DEA was still in the process of confirming the validity of the threat against me, there was nothing we could do but wait. Sit and wait; that was it for the time being. CeCe made a breakfast of egg sandwiches with avocado and bacon, one of my favorites for which I had absolutely no appetite, but I was able to choke down half of one with the help of three cups of coffee. However, Ingersoll ate three of the breakfast sandwiches with no problem; after all, he wasn't under any possible threat to his life.

CeCe went to her office to attempt to get some work done while I mostly made small talk with Detective Ingersoll to pass the time. I wasn't allowed to call into my office for obvious security reasons, no one needed to be aware of my whereabouts right now. As it turns out, Detective Dale Ingersoll actually did play college football and, get this, for the Fightin' Irish of Notre Dame, seven years earlier, all the while he earned a degree in criminology. He was a two-year starter there as a linebacker, and for whatever reason, I didn't recognize the name but should've.

He played in the NCAA Championship game in his senior year against Alabama, intercepting two passes and having twelve unassisted tackles. Unfortunately, they lost to the Crimson Tide as not many teams can make a claim to victory against the best team money can buy! Hey, I didn't make that up. I read that charge in several posts from the competition's alumni blogs, and you know that competing school's alumni are always spot on and accurate! The University of Alabama seems to attract a lot of the best high school prospects because of its stellar record for being a legitimate springboard into the NFL. Go figure; high school kids want to go where they get the best chance to get into the NFL. They might not be the sharpest tacks in the box, as my father would say, but they ain't quite as dumb as people may think they are.

Shortly after 1:00 p.m., Lieutenant Masters calls and tells me he would like to set up a three-way call at 2:00 p.m. with a member of the DEA to discuss what they have learned and how to proceed forward. Of course, this was the most agonizing hour of my life, and I can't say that CeCe felt any different even though she did her best to not show it. Promptly at 2:00 p.m., my phone rang, and Lieutenant Masters placed me on hold for a couple of minutes as he needed to make the connection to someone from the DEA the Drug Enforcement Administration. A United States federal law enforcement agency under the US Department of Justice tasked with combating drug trafficking and distribution within the United States. They have almost five thousand agents stationed throughout the country responsible for investigating violations of the controlled substance laws and regulations, bringing those responsible to the criminal and civil justice system of the US.

Now, while I tried a little marijuana, or "pot," as it was referred to in my time while I was back in college, I was never into the "drug scene" nor considered myself a regular user as it became to be known. For the most part, I was always extremely uncomfortable with that feeling of "being out of control" that so many seem to possess a strong desire and craving to experience. You could say I had "pot paranoia" when I smoked the stuff. Unfortunately, many people in our country, both young and old, have fallen deeply into this trap for whatever reason and, unfortunately, ruined their lives.

It is a chronic epidemic in our country, which has progressively gotten worse. Even many of those so-called "bright, intelligent, and well-educated" among us have been caught up in using illegal drugs and abusing prescription drugs. Many people admit that they began using drugs for recreational purposes based on a friend or family member's encouragement, only later to become severely addicted to the heavier stuff, which can easily overpower their common sense. Why so many continue to believe that they have this special power that they can control cravings whenever they want to just boggles my mind. It's called *addiction*, folks, and no one is immune even if you really believe you have a strong will and the desire to stop at any time.

Now, most recently, we hear about this drug called fentanyl, a controlled substance originally developed to treat severe pain, which is being used to lace other illegal and some prescription drugs to "trap" the user into desiring more. Obviously, drug traffickers see this as a huge advantage for selling more products to the end user, creating more demand for their product. Unfortunately, since illegal fentanyl is not regulated in any way, there is no way to tell how much of this drug is being used in the production process for the end user to know or control. Therefore, this has resulted in a very high number of overdose deaths than ever before since it can be fifty to a hundred times more powerful than heroin. No human can possibly survive that much strain on their body and live. As I said, this is just a sad part of our current American culture.

In my career as a human resources practitioner, I've had to deal firsthand with drug use on the job, continuing to be problematic. In short, this has been an organizational nightmare when employees come to work under the influence of drugs in their system. I'm not here to preach the evils of illegal drug use, but if you are just even halfway intelligent, all you need to do is wake up and see what is happening all around us and refuse to get involved in it. But as I have said many times, unfortunately, many people are like sheep, followers, and not independent thinkers. We all know of someone who has gotten caught up in this issue which also impacts the lives of others, family, friends, and even coworkers. It is truly a major problem in our society today.

Just then, Lieutenant Masters comes back on the line, "Mr. McCallister? Are you still there?"

"Yes, sir, I am here," I respond.

"Joe? Are you with us?" he asks.

"Hang on a sec, Dave. I have another call, won't take but a minute," a voice responds.

"Guess we're still holding, Mr. McAllister, sorry about that," Masters informs.

"Not a problem, I'm anxious to find out what's going on, but we'll wait until the agent is ready," I respond without any emotion.

"No choice here, but this is the man who will be able to give us some detail," Masters starts, "I will tell you that he doesn't believe that there's any real danger of someone coming after you because of the TV interview, but because of the informant's connection, the threat had to be confirmed."

"Oh, good to hear, but how can they be sure?" I ask.

Just then, the DEA agent comes back on the phone, "Sorry 'bout that, gentlemen, but I had to jump on that other call," the voice on the other end says.

"No prob, Joe," Masters announces, "I have Mr. McCallister on the other end, and he needs to know what you've already briefed me. I'm sure he wants to get on with his life, so Mr. McAllister, I'll turn this call over to DEA Special Agent Joseph Smith to give you an update."

Right then, I'm thinking, *Yeah, right, of course, this guy's real name is "Smith." Guess that's part of the undercover DEA agent game.*

"Good afternoon, I'm Special Agent Smith with the Drug Enforcement Agency, and I wanted to bring you current with what we first thought was a credible threat made on your life, sir, from a reliable source within an outside criminal group, which I cannot reveal at this time. An inside informant had sent a communications code suggesting that there was some discussion within the group that your name had been mentioned as a possible target based on the broadcast of a TV interview you were involved in yesterday. As of now, we don't believe this to be a cause for concern currently. The matter has not progressed any further as the informant has relayed that there is no further interest in pursuing the discussion within the organization. First, let me assure you that our inside informant is a deep plant within the organization and completely aware of all matters that would pertain to a potential threat of this nature. With this new information, we have removed the threat from code red at this time. We will get back in touch with Lieutenant Masters if anything changes however going forward, we believe everything is stable, and you have nothing to worry about, sir, do you have any questions?" Special Agent Joe Smith informs.

After a few seconds of allowing what I heard to sink into my brain, I begin, "So you feel confident that there is nothing to be concerned about right now, but how about going forward? Do I need to be looking over my shoulder every time I go out of my house?" I ask sarcastically.

"Sir, as I said," Agent Smith explains, "we truly believe everything associated with this matter is stable, there is no credible threat to you or anyone else associated with your company at this time. We cannot predict the future, but currently, you are not a target for this organization, but I understand your concern, and we will continue to monitor the situation to ensure no harm will transpire going forward," the agent replies.

"Can you guarantee that no harm will come of this going forward?" I ask.

"Unfortunately, no more than I can guarantee that you won't be in an automobile accident in the future," the agent retorts as I visualize a sly smile on his face.

"Okay, I guess I don't have any other option here but to take your word that I am under no threat at the current time but with no assurance going forward. I'll tell you, there's not much comfort in hearing that, especially since this all came to my attention just last night," I lament.

"I do understand, Mr. McAllister, and I want you to know that because of the credibility of our informant, learning that your name had been mentioned—and now it is no longer relevant to this organization—should give you some comfort that we have excellent information associated with this case. Perhaps, we shouldn't have jumped the gun and alerted you to this threat as soon as we did. However, it is always better to be safe now than sorry later. I apologize for the inconvenience you have experienced since the matter surfaced yesterday. Is there anything further you would like to ask?" the agent continues.

"Ah, no, Agent Smith, not at this time," I respond, "thank you for the update. It has been a very uneasy several hours for me and my wife, but thanks again.

With that, the phone call ended with Agent Smith, but I still wanted to hear from Lieutenant Masters on his take, so I asked if he would stay on the line.

"So, Lieutenant, are you convinced this is behind us now? It seems like it is being dismissed too quickly, how can the DEA be so sure this is really over for us?" I ask, testing his view.

"Well, Mr. McAllister," the police lieutenant starts, "we have no choice but to trust the DEA when it comes to this kind of thing. They are on top of this and most knowledgeable of what is happening in that world, but maybe if it will give you comfort, we can have an officer patrol your neighborhood on a regular basis. I cannot authorize Detective Ingersoll to continue his current on-sight assignment because of manpower restrictions, but hopefully, those seeing a patrol car regularly should be a potential deterrent."

As he is speaking, CeCe is vigorously shaking her head up and down.

"Okay, Lieutenant, if that's all that can be done, but I was hoping there was something else," I remark. "We'll look forward to having an officer patrol the immediate area more often, much appreciated."

We leave it at that, hoping this wasn't just lip service and that it will happen. However, I'm not convinced this will be a real deterrent for someone intent on taking me out; I don't believe most criminals aren't really that stupid, and if this truly coming from a drug cartel,

I don't think they give a damn about seeing a patrol car, occasionally cruising an area where they intend to commit a crime. That's just my thought, but maybe I'm wrong. Of course, I don't share this with CeCe; no need for her to have any concerns.

After wishing us well and leaving his contact information, Detective Ingersoll bids us goodbye with the best of luck. As the door closes, CeCe and I look at each in the eyes without saying a word and reach out to hold each other like there's no tomorrow. While we both share a huge feeling of relief, I still have doubts about this really being over for us. After all, there's still the obvious issue of what is really going on in the warehouse at Ocean Direct and how will management, which includes me, going to proceed forward to address the matter.

My God, if there's another drug ring operating in the warehouse, or worse yet, a drug cartel behind drugs being distributed out there, how will it go down for us? While talking to the DEA agent and Lieutenant Masters, I noticed Carl was trying to call me. So I dial Carl's number to let him know what has happened. He answered immediately, and after informing him of what the DEA agent revealed, he insisted that I should take a couple of days off to just get rebalanced. I reluctantly agree but let him know I have way too much going on to be out of the office any longer than that.

"Okay, Bill," Carl says, "but you know we're going to have to deal with whatever we have going on in that warehouse. We certainly don't need to have another drug operation going on out there, that's for sure."

"I totally agree, Carl, but we may need to bring in someone more qualified to help us deal with whatever is going on, I'm not so sure we can do this on our own," I suggest.

"Fine, Bill, fine, whatever it takes. We don't need any more negative publicity from the media either, so let's get together when you get back in and come up with a plan," Carl hangs up.

CeCe was very happy to hear I would be hanging around the house for the next few days instead of leaving her to go into the office. She is much more comfortable having me home for the next few days, and I will be glad to stay with her, just to be sure she will be okay.

As I think about everything I know at this point, I can't help but wonder why a drug cartel would have any concern about a company spokesperson mentioning eliminating drugs on the premises and identifying those responsible in a TV interview. Is this even worth their time? Why would this be a topic of conversation within their inner circle before an investigation has even been done? Obviously, like most reputable companies, we don't allow drugs or drug trafficking on our premises with a written policy to investigate the matter with law enforcement's assistance when reported. Every company has the same or a similar policy, and we certainly aren't the first to proudly proclaim that we don't tolerate this activity going on in our business. However, something doesn't completely add up, at least in my mind right now. Was this really an attempt to keep us from investigating the drug activity in the warehouse, or was it something else? However, it has become a big problem for ODI, but what is it all about? Somehow, I have a strange feeling that we will find out soon enough. Stay tuned!

Just another reason I keep asking myself, "Will I make it to the end?

While home for the next two days, Thursday and Friday, and still stun by the events of the week, CeCe and I didn't feel much like doing anything productive at all. She spends time in her office attempting to get some work done, but it seems like each time I stick my head in to see how she is doing, I find her staring out of her office window, deep in thought. Most of the time, I just sit around and listen to my favorite jazz music. There's something to be said about the funky sound of a good jazz artist that can sooth even the most stressful situation. Whenever I notice CeCe sitting idly at her desk, I have her lay with me on the couch and listen to the sweet sounds of Brian Culbertson, Paul Hardcastle, Vincent Ingala, and Diana Krall. This frequently resulted in both of us slipping off into nappy time as we were not yet sleeping through the entire night yet as our senses were still alerted to potential intruders for sure.

I would also have this occasional dream of someone pulling out an AK-47 or an Uzi and sending me to that eternal dirt nap! Because of this acute mental exhaustion, sometimes we just lay around and watch movies on Netflix, curled up on the couch. I couldn't tell you what we watched, so don't ask, and I don't think I even took a shower during this time; no wonder CeCe keeps her distance by the end of the second day! Hey, I didn't do anything remotely physical at all, so why would I need to bathe? That includes getting amorous with my loving wife, which is not even remotely on my mind, and I could tell she didn't exactly have an urge to engage in any "rumbling in the hay" either.

It was a very strange time indeed, just trying to mentally com-partmentalize the entire bad experience somewhere so that it made some sense. Of course, how do you rationalize the fact that someone told another someone that you should be a target for elimination just because you spoke your mind during a TV interview? And oh, by the way, I haven't even revealed how I really felt about the scumbags who poison our children and bring so much misery and pain to people with their illegal drug trafficking. If I had said anything like that, I would not be writing this book right now. Someone would be penning my obituary for sure. I have no doubt about that at all.

During this extended time together, CeCe and I had several intimate but completely necessary conversations about the experience we had just endured, and to some, it might not be a big deal, but we just needed to talk about it. I think it was what people do after they've experienced a traumatic type event in their lives, kind of like PTSD. All I know is that talking things through has helped us put the ordeal in the past, and now, the weekend is upon us. We were more than ready for some quality time with our friends. Man, was I looking forward to seeing these folks or what, even Charlie. Yep, even that sometimes "royal pain in the ass," as he often demonstrates. Oh crap, I just remembered; I owe him an explanation on why I couldn't talk the other day and why I did not call him back after I said I would. Oh great; I'm sure he thinks I blew him off when I cut the call short, but that's Charlie. Knowing him as I do, I'm pretty sure he's been pouting about it for the past couple of days. Well, this ought to be fun. I guess I will find out soon enough as we have our standing get-together with friends on Saturday night.

We arrived at Jack and Claire's just after seven on Saturday evening. As we walk up the driveway, CeCe whispers, "I don't see Charlie's or Janie's car, hmmm?"

I understand her implication as he is usually the first on the scene to get the party going. We walk in the front door to a broadly smiling Claire with her typical warm greeting, and I wave to Jack standing over by the bar. I notice Mark and Dave in a corner, and no doubt knee-deep in a political conversation, as Dave's body language indicates, but that doesn't stop Mark from momentarily looking up and yelling, "Hey, there, TV star!"

Jack approaches with a sly smile on his face and a glass of Four Roses for me and red wine for CeCe. As Claire takes CeCe by the arm and whisks her away, Jack says, "So Bill, we caught your bit on the news the other day. What the hell is going on down there at your workplace? Don't tell me you guys got drug dealers in your warehouse again?" he quips.

"Well, we're really not sure, Jack, still trying to figure that out," I reply, shrugging my shoulders.

"Well, you know what we would've done back when I was in corporate America, don't cha?" he asks.

"No, Jack, I don't know, but whatever you did, I'll bet it would be highly illegal today," I smile, which prompts a big belly laugh coming from the short, stocky, rotund host.

"By the way, where's Charlie and Janie? They are coming tonight, aren't they?" I ask, looking around.

"Sure, as far as I know, they certainly know the way here. But hey, you're right, usually Charlie comes early, you know, to get a jump on the libations, heh, heh," Jack muses.

I laugh and wonder if Charlie's absence is confirmation that he's still fuming over me cutting the call short with him the other day, which would be just like him. I see the girls all huddled out on the patio, so I walk over to say hello.

"Good evening, ladies," I say, approaching, "and how are we all doing this fine evening?"

They all respond that all is well, and then Steph asks how things are going down at my work, surely having a veiled reference to that now infamous TV interview with "Big Tits" Beth Spencer. I don't dare bring up anything about that in front of CeCe, as she is already on high alert to see who makes a comment about that hoity-toity TV anchor.

As is her standard fare, Claire has prepared a generous smorgasbord of finger foods and munchable delights on a table out by the pool. For some strange reason, suddenly, I am starving for something to eat, but I shouldn't be so surprised because I haven't eaten anything of substance since early this week as my appetite was almost non-existent. Perhaps my body is now craving some serious nutrients, and

I walk over to grab a plate and start helping myself to the goodies. I guess my mind is beginning to become more relaxed as well, obviously prompted by the bourbon in my hand and now my belly!

This is actually my first drink since Monday night when CeCe and I celebrated her new gig. And with that, the events of that night come streaming back into my mind; oh boy! I instinctively look over toward CeCe standing with the women, and I notice she is staring right at me with a huge smile on her face. I wink and smile back as my mind deliciously relives that night of romantic ravage we enjoyed before all that threat nonsense happened the next day. I know it may sound ridiculous, and I'm not usually one to believe in collaborative coincidences, but perhaps CeCe is having the very same warm thoughts of last Monday evening too! Well, let me tell you, there was no "maybe" about it; CeCe gives me her most seductive look and runs her wet tongue completely around her pouty lips as she dips her head and shoots the most innocent look in my direction. Whoa! Now I've got a strong urge to grab her by the hand and lead her into one of our hosts' bedrooms, and uh, I can't do that, not right now anyway. We'll just have to pick this up later and turn this mental dance of romance into action when we get back home. Talk about a genuine connection with another person; we most definitely have that for sure and more!

Just then, I hear Charlie's booming voice as he and Janie come striding through the front door.

"Hey, folks, the king is here, now the party can begin," he proclaims as he enters with a glass full of some clear liquid, which I know is not water and assumes it's white liquor, vodka, or maybe white rum.

Okay, so he's already got a head start on the evening, nothing new for him, but at least he usually waits until he arrives at his destination. God, I hope Janie drove them over here but knowing her as I do, of course, she did. Charlie heads straight to the bar to greet Jack, leaving Janie standing there alone by the front door. I notice Claire heading over to grab her, but that's Charlie for you; he lives to be the life of the party, even if that means he has little consideration for his bride. I'm still baffled at how long they've been able to stay together;

God, that woman is unbelievable! I focus on Charlie and notice he's stopping to greet everyone else in the place and hasn't even looked over my way.

Okay, so this is how it's going to be tonight. Charlie will ignore me for a while as he "gets me back" for the other day. Talk about immature insecurity; we've known each other for more than fifty years, yet he still doesn't believe I have his back? Guess I will have to apologize at some point tonight, and best to get it over sooner than later, or else the "party master" does something stupid and embarrassing. I walk over to greet him as he and Dave are chatting about how hot the weather has been lately.

"Hey, man," I say, extending my hand, "glad you could make it, we were wondering when you guys were going to get here."

Just then, I notice this fiery rage in his eyes that I don't ever recall before, and suddenly Charlie has grabbed me up by the waist and is literally carrying me across the patio. I'm pushing down on his shoulders, dropping my glass of bourbon on the pool deck, a colossal waste of good booze. But to no avail, I can't break free of his grip, and then Charlie throws me right into the pool! As I sink into the chlorine water, I can hear a couple of women screaming and Jack yelling Charlie's name. I'm trying to understand what the hell just happened as I surface to a standing position. Even for Charlie, this is uncharacteristic, unexpected, and completely insane.

Jack and Dave run over and grab him by the arms, getting right up into his face and simultaneously yelling what the hell are you doing, and what's the matter with you? Charlie just pushes them away and goes over and sits in a pool chair and places his head in his hands with his arms on his knees.

Dave follows him, still barking at him, "Are you crazy?" he yells, "answer me! What is wrong with you?"

Charlie just sits there with his head down and looks dazed and confused. Meanwhile, Mark reaches out, offering a hand to help me out of the pool. CeCe runs over and grabs my arm, asking if I am okay?

"Of course," I respond, "I'm fine, just wet and pissed."

Claire comes quickly with a stack of towels as I shoot a menacing look over toward Charlie. "Now, just be calm, Bill, no need to get upset," CeCe says as she starts drying me off with a large towel.

"Too late for that," I mutter and walk over to Charlie, where Dave is still trying to get a response from Charlie.

"Hey, man, not cool!" I yell, "why'd you do that, you idiot!"

Just then, Janie comes over, bending down toward Charlie, yelling, "I told you not to do this tonight, how embarrassing!" Which was very surprising to all of us, we had never even heard her raise her voice at Charlie ever before. You go, girl!

Just then, Charlie looks up at me and says, "I thought we were friends, Bill," and he starts sniffling, which completely stops everyone in their tracks. Other than his sniffles, you could literally hear a pin drop as I was now aware of the pool filter hum.

"What are you talking about?" I began, "you're still upset that I couldn't talk to you the other day, well, what you don't know is that I had something more important at that very moment that was—"

I didn't finish as Charlie interrupted me, "Yes, I know all about the threat on your life, Bill, that's what I'm upset about. We've known each other all these years, and you didn't think this was something that you could tell me? You couldn't confide in me at all? I had to find out myself that my best friend in the whole world was being threatened and that the fucking cops were staying at your house to make sure you were safe, that's what I'm talking about," Charlie sobbed. "I just thought we were closer than that, Bill, guess I was dead wrong, sorry, poor choice of words."

"What's all this about?" Dave asks.

"Yeah, what's going on, Bill?" Mark pipes up.

Right then, I have a strong desire to have another drink as it sharply occurs that I have some explaining to do as Ricky Ricardo from the I Love Lucy show used to quip when he was upset with her antics. But before I can get another word out of my mouth after gesturing toward Jack that I'd like to have another drink, CeCe begins to speak in her most animated and loudest possible voice, "Look, folks, Bill was notified by the police that because of some comments he gave to the TV station about not tolerating drug activity on his company's premises, which is an appropriate response to a stupid interviewer's question, a threat of harm toward Bill was picked up by an informant with the DEA, who apparently was planted inside a known drug cartel. As it turned out, the threat was later dismissed as unconfirmed, it was eliminated by the DEA, and the police protection was discontinued. However, we were explicitly told to not share any information about this with anyone, even other family members, as a matter of fact, we haven't even told the kids and have no plans to do that any time soon either. And Charlie, I'm surprised that you, you of all people, don't have enough confidence in Bill to know when it is appropriate for him to share information with you. You are very well aware that his job deals primarily in confidential matters affecting other people, and he is not at liberty whatsoever to openly discuss things of this nature with anyone, especially sensitive information like this! What is wrong with you? You get your feelings hurt because he doesn't tell you about something that has absolutely nothing to do with you, and then you throw him into a pool because you think he doesn't care about you? You have a serious problem, Charlie, and you need help, thank you very much for showing all of us your ass tonight and behaving like a completely spoiled child," she ends with, "God help you, Charlie, you certainly need it!"

No one said a word or even dared to interrupt her as she completed her rant. Talk about hearing a pin drop now; I think that would've been a welcomed event, especially to Charlie. For that, I am sure he stopped sobbing and even displayed a sobering look on his face.

As I stood there dripping wet, I could not have felt prouder of my wife as I ever did than any other time; even Janie smiled and came over and put her arm around CeCe. That's when I noticed CeCe was breathing a little heavier than usual; I guess a display of emotion like this can do that to anybody, even my usually cool, calm, and collected wife! Thankfully, Jack had a pair of swim trunks that fit my slenderer frame, and I had another shirt in the car that I carried for emergencies. Of course, they didn't match, but no one really cared as the mood was somewhat depressed after the unexpected excitement we just went through. Needless to say, the night was looking like it was going to be a complete bust and could end early at any moment as the tension was uncomfortably evident; that is until Mark felt compelled to make a compassioned speech. He began by proclaiming that what we had witnessed this evening was just a perfect example of how close our little group of friends had become. He went on to say that we have always been comfortable in our own skins, able to speak our minds on any topic, and it was obvious that even a genuine misunderstanding shows exactly how much love and care was among our group.

Now, Mark was in the sales field, currently working for a small pest control company in charge of their corporate accounts. He had bounced around in various sales positions over the years, and even though he had held several different jobs, they had all been for more than five years each. He was a real nice guy, but maybe not as driven as Charlie, Jack, or me. Charlie and I knew Mark from college when we hung out together between classes and partied on occasion. Actually, I'm responsible for introducing Mark to his wife, Deb, after knowing her from a class we had together. It was instant head-over-hills love for Mark, but it took Deb a while to come around to him as he was not the most expressive guy and was always nervous around girls back then.

Mark was definitely low-key by nature, and that might explain why he never stayed in one job for any long period of time. Sales can be a brutal dog-eat-dog profession unless you are a constantly high producer or you are well connected. As an introvert, Mark did not cultivate many lasting connections even though he was a high producer taking his work seriously, but without that killer drive for success, he eventually found himself unhappy when he was constantly passed over for promotions time after time. I've counseled Mark on his career for many years, and while he has the heart and desire to be the best he can be, he struggles with staying focused and setting defined goals for success. Therefore, he has not yet reached his true potential and most likely won't before he retires. He and Deb have two grown children who were good friends with our kids, Jimmy and Olivia, growing up together in our small town. On several occasions, we had them over and vice versa, getting together for the kids as they became really good friends; they all stayed connected through the years.

Therefore, it was somewhat surprising that he would be the one to try and save the evening tonight, but you know what, maybe he had this ability within him all along and just needed the right catalyst to coax it out. No matter though, what he said to our group in his speech came across in such a healing way that you could feel an immediate turn in the tide to the mood, and it made perfect sense to all of us. Even Charlie, yes, even that self-absorbed clown alcoholic, began to lose the frown and obvious guilt of ruining it for everyone. His body language and face showed the hope and promises we were seeking that all would be well for the balance of the evening. Later, he even clanked his glass and gave a sincere apology to the entire group for his inappropriate behavior, focusing all the while on me, offering to let me throw him in the pool as retribution for his actions. Although I can't say for sure that any of this was truly heartfelt or sincere; perhaps it was the vodka or whatever the hell he had in that glass, but something was prompting his confession, and none of us really cared.

In any event, the rest of the evening went much better than we thought it would earlier, and we didn't have or want to cut it short. Of course, Dave and I had to help Charlie into the car for Janie as he was out of it, as usual, by the end of the night. As CeCe and I drove home that night, I told her that while I was extremely proud of her for sticking up for me as she did, I didn't want her to ever do that again.

"What? Why, Bill," she cried, "I thought it was the right thing to do under the circumstances, and I knew you weren't in the mood to explain anything about the threat, and when I saw the serious look of anger for Charlie you had on your face." She glanced over, seeing me with this huge grin and lifting my eyebrows teasingly. "Oh God, you ass," she says and hits me on the upper arm.

"Ow, that hurt, CeCe," I teasingly complain. "But it was worth it just to hear you say it again." I laugh.

"I'll show you hurt, buster," she replies, "you just wait till we get home." She fake-laughed back at me.

The next day, Sunday was more of a day of relaxation and, of course, pleasantly filled with a nice memory of our romantic escapade from the night before. Hey, sex three times within a week? And this included dealing with a possible threat of harm; go figure! Maybe I should get myself threatened more often if it would create an increase in our sexual opportunities! *Not!* That being said, I am looking forward to getting back to work tomorrow as I have a lot on my plate already, and now, we have this situation in the warehouse that will need to be addressed. I really didn't want to do anything today, but I went ahead and jotted down some general ideas for the meeting with Carl tomorrow as I was certain he will be asking for some contribution from his inner circle. Whew, this past week has been a whirlwind of different emotions and activity, and as unsettling as all that was, I have no idea what is about to transpire, a lot sooner than I could ever imagine.

Oh God, it's already Monday once again, and my head is filled with dread as I walk through the hallways toward the HR offices. The drive-in was better than usual, but I didn't leave at my usual time; of course, I'm milking my extended time off as long as possible. So what? I'm getting here for work at ten instead of eight; what are they gonna do? Fire me? Please, do me a favor and put me out of my misery. Making my way toward my office, I noticed that almost everyone I come across seems to be too busy talking on their telephones or concentrating on their computer screens with their heads down, but it sure feels obvious they're are going out of their way to ignore my presence, almost like on purpose. Everyone that is, except Rosie; as I enter the outer door into the HR department, she looks in my direction and jumps up from her seat.

"Well, good morning Mr. McCallister," as she followed me into my office. "How was your fishing trip?" she asks.

"Fishing trip?" I respond a bit confused, not breaking stride.

"Yes, Mr. Johnson sent out a memo the other day to everyone here in HR that you were taking a few days off to get in some fishing, a well-deserved special event," she states as we entered my office.

Okay, I was thinking Carl must have thought that my staff needed an explanation for my absence since it was unusual for me to just not show up at the office and disappear for a couple of days.

"Uh, yes, it was fine, thank you, Rosie. Was everything okay here while I was out? Any problems?" I ask, wishing I probably shouldn't have.

"No, sir, no big issues, all was well," she replies. "We had to deal with the police while you were away, but Sarah handled their requests, they just wanted to look at some personnel file," she went on. "Too bad about Rafael, huh?" she adds.

"Okay, Rosie, what's going on with Rafael? I thought he didn't want to pursue anything further with the beating from the thugs last week. He even refused to get medical treatment, is he okay?" I press.

"Uh, well, he's been suspended from work, and Mr. Milken wanted me to have you call him as soon as you got in this morning," she mumbles.

"Suspended? What for?" I ask.

"Well, Sarah said Mr. Milken really wanted to fire him, but she told him that he couldn't do that until after he talked with you first, so he was suspended until the investigation into what happened the other morning is concluded," she replies.

"What? Why would we fire the guy who was beaten up by outside intruders without completing a thorough investigation of all the facts? Get Sarah in here as soon as possible, Rosie, and oh, by the way, have my phone routed to your desk for the balance of the morning please, thank you," I direct.

"Yes, sir, but it already is, and I have a few phone messages, which I can go over whenever you're ready, and then there's this employee committee who said they really need to meet with you as soon as you are available, something about a merit increase program they were working on that—" she goes on.

"Rosie! Please, get Sarah in here!" I interrupt abruptly.

"Yes, sir." With that, she turns and leaves my office. Without a minute, Sarah comes hurrying in.

"Good morning, sir, I know you want an update on the warehouse issues, but just so you know, suspending Rafael was my fallback position as John was adamant about terminating him immediately," she blurts out.

"Sarah? On what basis did we have to suspend Rafael?" I ask with concern.

"Well, the way I saw it, he did refuse to cooperate with the police and wouldn't talk to us either, John or me, at all. And he refused to fill out an incident report as well," she explains.

"Okay, but," I slow my speech, "did anyone think that maybe he was threatened about saying anything to anybody about what happened to him?" I explain. "Or could he have been in shock?" I roll my eyes. There was a brief pause in the exchange as I could see Sarah was processing my words. "Okay, what's done is done, Sarah, I understand you were under the gun with John, so maybe having him stay home until we get to the bottom of things is best for now. We can always reinstate him and pay back wages for the time missed later. I'll talk with Milken this morning, and we'll figure out the next step, but I really don't think termination is appropriate, that's ridiculous, we have absolutely nothing to base that on at this point," I say adamantly.

Before leaving my office, Sarah brought me up to date on the police requests; they wanted to see if there were any connections Rafael had listed in his contacts. Sometimes, a connection to criminal activity is made by who the victim admits knowing as most crimes frequently happen in small circles, and there's no honor among thieves, as they say. According to my information, the police solve many of their cases through learning about the various connections with others related to family or friendships. It's those isolated incidents that involve total strangers where most of the cold cases go unsolved.

I pick up my phone to dial Milken's extension but not without reservation. I already know where he's coming from on this matter.

"John, this Bill. You wanted to discuss the situation with Rafael and the incident the other day?" I ask.

After a brief hesitation, he starts, "Yeah, I do…uh, I think we just need to go ahead and let him go. He's not one of my best workers, and with this last incident, I don't believe he's good to have around the warehouse anymore. Nobody likes him anyway, and I wouldn't be shocked if it was him who put the drugs in that cleaning storage cabinet. I'm sure those idiots who came in here and beat his ass weren't happy he lost their drugs. Besides, he refuses to talk about what happened, and he won't fill out an incident report, we can fire him just for that, right?" John demands.

"Okay, John, I understand the urgency to do something in response to the incident the other morning, but right now, we have absolutely no evidence to back up terminating an employee who was a victim of a crime on our premises. Do you understand how big of a mistake that might turn out to be, which we could be handing an attorney who might decide to take the case if he chooses to seek legal action?" I respond.

"What? That loser isn't going to file a lawsuit if we fire him, he's too stupid, and by the way, since he won't talk to the police or even his employer about who did this to him, he'll be afraid they'll come to get his ass again. Look, Bill, I know it's your job to protect the company from legal action, but in this case, this nobody is not going to risk doing that because he knows it's not in his best interest or his health. Trust me on this one, he needs to go, and that's the bottom line. I only agreed to suspend him because your woman over there said you needed to okay the termination. What else do I need to do to make this happen, tell me, and I'll do it, but he's gotta go—" he rants.

Finally, I interrupt, "John, John, listen to me, I know how you feel, but we do not have any proof that Rafael is involved in anything drug-related right now, and we have nothing else to be able to defend against a wrongful termination court case. There are literally hundreds of labor attorney's out there just waiting for a case like this to come up, a Latino male with no documented job performance problems who was brutally beaten while on the job, and we're going to terminate his employment for no good reason? I'm not in favor of that, besides, who's to say the kid is not still in shock, and that's why he refused to fill out the incident report last week," I try to reason.

"Ah, bullshit," he screams. "This is nothing but you and your department wanting to play God over my department and my employees. I'm capable of making my own decisions without interference from your department, whether you believe that or not. I'll talk to Sam Morris about this, and if necessary, I'll take this to Carl, and I'm sure he'll agree with me." With that, he hangs up.

I'm not worried about talking to Carl about this, and I feel pretty confident he will support my recommendation. I have no plans to bother Carl with this, nor do I run to him with these kinds of employee matters; he has bigger fish to fry, and besides, John may not follow through with his veiled threat anyway.

I knew before I dialed John's number this conversation was not going to go well. John Milken is a complete arrogant blockhead who doesn't understand that he just can't do anything he wants to do and whenever he wants to do it without following the rules and getting another opinion, especially when it involves employees of ODI. However, he's convinced that whatever he wants, and when faced with someone is in his way, all he needs to do is scream and rant, and then everyone falls in line. If that doesn't sound like a man who hasn't completely moved on from his stint in the military, then I've apparently mistaken the obvious behavior. But it's entirely possible that I have John all wrong, so then he becomes nothing more than just a royal supreme asshole! I think I like that definition better.

CeCe answers the phone, expecting me to check in to see how her day has gone, when instead, she recognizes a familiar voice say, "Well, hello, how are you today?" Charlie asks.

Somewhat surprised, CeCe responds, "Charlie, you know you're not supposed to call me anymore, we had an agreement."

"Cecelia, this isn't a call about us, well, not entirely, but it's not about what happened between us previously. I've moved on, and I know you have too," Charlie explains.

"Okay, what's this about? Last night?" CeCe asks.

"Uh, well, I just wanted to say, you were very hurtful to me in front of all our friends, and while I understand you were defending your man but did you have to add the emotion and make me out to be a complete jerk in the process?" he protests.

"Look, Charlie, you didn't have to throw Bill in the pool," she yells. "That was completely and totally unnecessary and was humiliating to him and me. Our friends didn't appreciate the antics one bit, even coming from you, that was wrong," She laments.

"Okay, I get it," he said, "maybe it was a bit much, but you make it sound like I hit him in the face, I just tossed him in the pool, that's all. No harm, no foul, and I was just angry that he didn't tell me anything about the threat. Not one word, and I'm supposed to be his best friend. Oh, by the way, neither did you, for that matter," he went on.

"Charlie, what happened between us was a big mistake, and anything having to do with you does not include having any more contact or even the premise of a connection, do you get that? And we should not be talking about this at all, it's been over for years and way in the past. If Bill were to ever find out what happened, it would be the end of any friendship with you and destroy two marriages for that, I am sure," CeCe scolds.

"Cecelia, I know what we had a while ago was not right, and I am well aware that it's over, you've made that quite clear. I haven't bothered you about it anymore, not in the last five years at least," he replies.

"Okay then, it's over and in the past, so just forget about last night. I had to show Bill that I was appalled at your behavior, and I was not going to tolerate it. What? Did you want him to punch you in the face? Surely, you saw the look on his face," she continues, "So let's end this conversation right now, never to discuss it again."

"But Cecelia," he begins, "what happened between us is forever etched in my brain, and even though you decided it was over, I can't help but—"

"Charlie, stop it! This is gone on for too long, we never should've gotten involved. It's over and has been over for some time. If this continues, you are risking us being found out for what we did, and that will ruin a lot of good people's lives. Do you hear me, Charlie?" CeCe adamantly shouts.

"Okay, okay, I won't mention this again, and I promise not to bother you anymore. If that's what you really want?" Charlie responds.

"Yes, Charlie, it is most definitely what I want. So please do not call my number again. I can be cordial with you when we are with our friends, but I will never show any sign that we ever had anything together in front of them and, for sure, not Bill. So good-bye, Charlie," She hangs up the phone, knowing that extending the conversation only gives him an opportunity to continue his case.

The leadership team met with Carl to discuss the events of the warehouse, and even though the other directors listened intently to the conversation, which volleys back and forth between me, Carl, and Sam Morris, it seemed like this was not a subject any of the others had much to contribute. Obviously, they all had their own issues, and after all, this was a problem currently isolated in the warehouse at this time. So without any firm decisions from this waste of time meeting, Carl left it up to me to work with the police to see if we could come up with an action plan that he could endorse. Therefore, the rest of my day was filled with Sarah and I commandeering the HR conference room to go through all the information from the incident and calling the police department to ensure we were playing with the same deck of cards, so to speak.

When it came time to leave for the day, I felt exhausted, trying to determine a course of action that be acceptable to Carl; however, we did agree that adding more security personnel to that cesspool out there would be necessary and absolutely essential if we wanted to prevent a potential negligence charge emerging from an employee should there be another event such as the one that occurred last week.

My drive home that evening was consumed with my thoughts of what else we might do to change the culture that exists out there, and I kept coming back to replacing John Milken as he was the common denominator to the constant problems. Just before I pulled into my driveway, I got an epiphany. What if I convinced Carl that we should do an anonymous employee satisfaction survey with the employees; perhaps that might reveal some information that could lead us to who they suspect are the troublemakers and drug culprits. John might even be okay with this as it might implicate Rafael, which could be the smoking gun, and justify taking action against the person he believes to be our drug problem. Then again, it might also exonerate him, which would be okay with me but would infuriate Milken, but I'm definitely all right if it goes that way as it could shut him up for a little while anyway. Still, Carl will need to buy into this as he will think I'm just looking for more ammo to hold up against John. Well, maybe that did cross my mind, but it isn't the primary objective here. No, certainly not. That's my story, and I'm sticking to it!

CeCe and I have a quiet dinner and watch a little TV before retiring to bed, but I sense that she has something on her mind that she's not telling me, so when she climbs into bed, I ask, "Baby, what's going on with you tonight? You haven't said more than a few words since I got home. Did something happen today, you're not telling me?"

She quickly snaps that nothing happened, but it wasn't what she said, but it was the manner in which it came out. So I reach over and put my arm around her and say, "CeCe, you're too obvious, and you make a bad liar, I can tell that you are bothered by something. If you don't want to talk about it right now, I won't press the issue, but please, just know that I'm here when you want to talk."

She leans over and kisses my cheek and softly says, "Bill, it's okay, it's probably nothing. I'm just concerned that all this crap that's going on with your job and that messed-up warehouse is stressing you out. This is not good for your health, and you're so close to retirement. I don't want you to come down with any serious problems from this job right before you leave it. It's not worth it, I'm doing very well with my work, and we are financially fine. If you felt like you wanted to go ahead and retire, I would have no objection, I just want us to have several good years ahead of us."

"Of course, and I do too," I assure her, "but you know I need to complete my final two years for the 100 percent retirement benefit and whatever contributions go into my 401(k) account for the company match. Besides, I made a commitment to the company and Carl, even if I left now, I haven't even groomed a replacement, and it will take some time to do that anyway."

"Bill, you know good and well Sarah is more than ready to step into your job, you've trained her very well, and again, we don't need the money, we have plenty for what we need. The house is almost paid off, and if we sell it to relocate closer to Olivia, David, and the kids, we will downsize and buy a cozy place that costs less, we'll be able to pay cash," she pleads as she has it all figured out.

"Okay, CeCe, we'll discuss this further, but right now, I have a problem in the warehouse that requires my full attention, and I can't focus on the future until I resolve the present," I respond, knowing full well that sooner or later, we're going to have to discuss this plan she has for our future. I realize that it will not be well received, but I'm trying to put the discussion off as long as possible because I'm sure it will put a big strain on our relationship as this is all she had talked about since she began her own business; it has been her vision, and I have not openly disagreed to it yet. "Good night, honey," I say and turn over, facing the opposite wall.

"Good night, my love," CeCe responds, and with that, we both slip off into our nightly dreamworlds.

Far away in the fog of my mind, I hear a repetitive buzzing that gets louder on each successive occurrence. Suddenly, I realize it's my phone ringing on the night stand. What time is it and who could this be? I glance at the alarm clock—it reads 4:15. 4:15? Immediately, my somewhat disoriented mind goes to wondering if something has happened to one of the kids. I pick up the phone and squint my eyes to focus—it's Sarah! *What the hell is she calling me at this hour for?* I'm thinking as I press the answer button.

"Hello? Sarah, what is it? What's happened?" I mouth as I clear my throat.

"I'm so sorry to bother you, Mr. McCallister, but we have a big problem, I just got a call from our night security office at the plant, and there's been a shooting in the warehouse. Apparently, someone has shot Alice Randle in the parking lot when she went out to her car," Sarah blurts all in one breath. "They have no idea who did it, the police are there, I just thought you would want to know right away. I'm not sure what we need to do." She was rambling.

"Hold on, Sarah. Just a sec," I interrupt her as I sit up and put on my glasses and flip on the nightstand lamp.

"Okay, slow down now. Take a deep breath," I try to say as calmly as possible still clearing my foggy head.

By this time, CeCe is grabbing my arm and asking what's going on. "Who is it?"

"Okay, where is Alice now?" I ask, anticipating the worst.

"I'm sorry, Mr. McCallister, I just got the call a few minutes ago. I'm just so upset. Apparently, she's on her way to the hospital."

I hear the seriousness in Sarah's voice. "It's okay, Sarah. It's going to be all right," I respond as calmly as I can.

"Should I go to the hospital, or what do you want me to do?" she asks excitedly.

"Sarah, I'm going to get ready and head to the office now. I will call you on the way. Just meet me there as soon as you can. Give me about twenty minutes, and I will call you right back." I click off the phone and look up at CeCe who is now standing right in front of me with her hand on my shoulder.

"What happened, Bill? is someone hurt at work? Is something bad going on there? What is it?" she asks.

I respond slowly, "I'm not sure, babe. I don't have the details yet, but it looks like we've had a shooting with one of our warehouse workers in the parking lot. I need to get down there right away." I rise from the bed head toward the bathroom and turn on the shower.

CeCe comes in the bathroom and grabs my arm and pulls me to her. "Now? You have to go right now? It's four o'clock in the morning, what do you think you can do at this hour?" she asks. "Just let the police handle this for now and…and Sarah can go in your place." CeCe's concern is clear and present. Even though I look directly into her eyes, it's even obvious to me that my vision is just a gaze.

"CeCe, I have no idea what I can do, but I just need to get there as soon as possible. I will be all right. Besides, it's my job, and the traffic will be light at this hour. I can be there in forty minutes. I'm sure the police have everything under control, but right now, there are some very upset team members, no doubt. Maybe me just being there will be comforting to them, I don't know. I just need to go," I proclaim, trying to halfway convince myself it is what I need to do. I really don't have a clue what I can do or even what I should do but just go and be present.

As I step quickly into the shower. My mind is all over the place—how can this happen? At my workplace? Under my watch? What the hell is going on? I start to get dressed, CeCe heads into the kitchen to brew some coffee. As I pull my shoes on and stand, I can't help but wonder what was thought to be just an unhappy employee over a missed promotional opportunity, must actually go deeper than that—much deeper. Little did I know just how deep this really was.

* * *

I glance my watch. It's 5:15, and the sun has yet to show its smiling face. I head the car toward the office, a trip I've made a thousand and one times, wondering if a day like this might happen before I traded my work clothes for those comfortable shorts and t-shirt. Sure, it has crossed my mind on several occasions that something like this could happen. Because people are people, and I've definitely seen my fair share of crazy behavior from employees over the years. But did I really think it would ever come to this, in my workplace?

I dial Sarah's number, not really knowing what to expect but hoping for the best. Sarah answers quickly, but I can hear a lot of commotion in the background and I can tell she is outside.

"Hello, Mr. Mac, I hope you can hear me. I'm in the parking lot talking with some team members to find if they might have seen something else they didn't tell the police. They're all concerned about Alice and it's not a good situation and there's blood all over the place. Oh my God, it's everywhere, Mr. Mac. This is terrible, and I'm not sure what we can do to calm them down. John Milken is here, and he seems to be the most upset," she says with alarm.

I started to tell Sarah to just be calm as possible and tell the employees that everything is being handled by the police, but before I could get half of that out, I hear John Milken screaming, "Is that McCallister on the phone, give me that," he shouts.

"McCallister, are you on the way here? What the hell are you going to do about this? This is all HR's fault. You people made me promote this woman knowing it wasn't gonna make a lot of my employees happy, and now we have this mess to deal with, I wish you guys would just stay out of my warehouse from now on. I hope you're happy now!"

Now John and I have never been close and at times it's been a very strained relationship, to say the least. Even back when I first started with ODI, John never officially welcomed me to the company. I think he knew right from the start that I was not going to be his ally when it came to how he had the warehouse for all those years previous to my arrival. The good ol' boys club, as the atmosphere out there was described to me and confirmed when John Milken was introduced to me. I knew it was not going to be easy to effect change in that warehouse given the history, but I had hoped that in this modern day and time, it wouldn't be met with so much resistance. Wow, was I so wrong. It has been a real challenge, and on several occasions, John and I have butted heads in executive meetings, even over operational issues having nothing to do with employee behavior or his archaic management style. Apparently, we are just like oil and water and rarely see eye-to-eye on much of anything, especially employment decisions dealing with strategic direction for warehouse operations. Clearly, we've seen our working relationship as adversarial, at best. It was so apparent to other leaders in the company that jokes were made when there was an issue, they knew John and I would differ, which was quite often.

Mr. Johnson even spoke with me about the tension between John and I a few years ago. he advised that I should be the bigger of the two since I was at a higher-level in the company reporting to the CEO. John was not seen as a strategic decision-maker even though he knew everything there was to know about warehouse operations; no one expected him to make a major impact on the company from his position. On the other hand, I was there to model and demonstrate ideal behavior and be the change agent for making the company the best it can be from the employee's perspective. Johnson never doubted me or my abilities so he didn't seem concerned about my role, he was just giving me some "Dutch uncle" advice—don't get caught up in the archaic beliefs of those who did not see the future and who were not the future of ODI.

There was this event that occurred back roughly seven years ago at an annual company management dinner with our spouses that just seemed to be very odd to me. For some reason, and I have a feeling that it was intentional, that John and his wife were seated at the same table as CeCe and I with two other couples. Coincidental? I think not. The previous admin assistant to the CEO, before we found Jayne

Davis, responsible for seating arrangements at this annual awards dinner, I believe had deliberately put both John and I at the same table. Why? Well, there was no official reason that I could determine at the time, but it has dawned on me recently that maybe someone, like our fearless leader, felt like we might soften our feelings about each other especially with our pleasant wives present. CeCe had been always well-received by my work colleagues as she was the most gracious of all of the other significant others, at least I my mind anyway. But actually, I have received many compliments from the executive staff as CeCe, while not a social butterfly, was always kind and cordial to everyone. Besides, that killer smile of hers would always immediately disarm anyone who even thought about disagreeing with her. On top of that, CeCe was a great-looking woman for her sixty-two years of age. She always kept her herself in good shape, not in a fanatical way, but just you can tell when a person takes pride in themselves. Not pretentious, not obnoxious, and certainly not arrogant, CeCe was the consummate partner in every way. Again, I routinely go back to admitting that I definitely married above my pay grade, and while she would never say that or ever make me feel that, I know the truth and I'm okay with it! Yes, I am VERY okay with that!

Now John's wife, Maria, was an outspoken, very opinionated woman whose family was originally from Venezuela. She was an attractive woman, but every time I ever saw her, usually at these annual management functions, she always wore excessive make-up, most likely to belie years. It was a second marriage for both John and Maria, and they had only been together for a short period of before the dinner meeting. They met a few years after their original spouses passed away within months of each other. They had joined a dating website and met online within a relatively quick period of time—a kind of a rebound type relationship, I always thought. After they were married, there was several comments made that it just did not seem like these two were that compatible. John, being the gruff, old-school, quiet but very set in his ways southern man, and this elegant and gaudy type foreign-born lady just did not seem to match in a lot of ways. Her English was okay, but there were times when she became emotional that it was difficult to understand her enunciations clearly. But who should be allowed to pass judgment on two people who found something special enough to make the decision to get married? Needless to say, CeCe and I were not invited to the wedding as most all the other executives in the company were there. There was some lame excuse afterward that our invitation was mailed out and came back returned to sender for an incorrect address, of course, after the wedding. Did I really care? I'm not sure I would've had a wonderful time, but CeCe insisted on getting them a wedding gift anyway…which is just like her. Maria had called her up and thanked her profusely for the gift, a set of crystal glassware with their initials engraved in gold inlay. However, as CeCe tells it, there was something very strange about the phone call, she said it seemed obligatory and not really genuine at all. And that's saying something for CeCe to put it in those words, since she believes everyone always has the truest of intentions, much like herself. But as I mentioned, no invite to this event was not a problem for me as I did not have to go and pretend to want to be there anyway.

At that annual management dinner a few years ago, with John and I at the same table with our spouses and the two other couples, everyone was on their best behavior. It was a bit uncomfortable at least in the beginning, with John and I not saying much to each other. However, as the wine continued to flow, Maria became louder with her voice and started talking about how John and first met. No one had asked that question, but I guess she felt compelled to explain their situation. I wasn't paying much attention to her as she talked about their online romance until she mentioned something about John and her were going to try to conceive a child. What? Now, John is a bit older than me, and at that specific time, he was in his midfifties and his other children were already grown on their own. Maria, although she looked much older and did not have any children, was in her forties, certainly an advanced age for someone considering childbirth, in my opinion.

Once she made that comment, John immediately announced that nothing had been decided, but they were just considering it. Based on the look of surprise from the other couples and CeCe and I, John's next comment prompted the customary raised eyebrows around the table. He followed up his initial statement about considering childbirth with a definitive remark that this was Maria's wish and he was not "onboard" yet. Oh boy, he might as well have lit a firecracker at the table because Maria went off on him like a roman candle on New Years' Eve! She began hollering and screaming at him like he was a dog—at which time every jaw hit the table. Really? This is what they're going to do? Argue about having a child at our annual management meeting dinner? In front of all of us? All righty then, as the HR person, I had no choice but try to calm the situation by asking Maria in my most delicate and low-key way to please lower her voice, settle down, and if she and John needed to excuse themselves, it might be best. At which time, John barked at her to "shut up and just act like you have manners, even if you don't," he bellowed. Well, wasn't this pleasant? A full-blown marital dispute right out in the open in front of everyone, and so loud everyone that three tables nearest us heard them too. Why should I be surprised, or better yet, why didn't I see this coming?

Well, with that, Maria did leave but John did not, and as a matter of fact, he grabbed another glass of wine from the waiter's tray and inhaled it all in one large gulp. Now, wine is not supposed to be consumed that way; he wasn't drinking it for the flavor or the texture or the ambiance. He was looking to drown a bad feeling with alcohol—any alcohol—and the wine was the closest thing he could get his hands on. Of course, that was temporary as John then got up from the table and headed off in the direction Maria went. No doubt, everyone thought he was going to go console Maria after his very inappropriate comments. Well, at least that's what we all thought, anyway. However, shortly following John's departure, Maria returned to the table and sat down asking if we knew where John was. Uh, well…Not knowing how to answer her since John did not announce his intentions when he left, we all shrugged our shoulders in unison. It then became clearly evident that there were some serious kinks in that marriage of short-lived history which did not come as a surprise at all to anyone at the table.

Now, I'm not usually an angry person even when it comes to someone who is making unfounded, irrational, and ridiculous accusations about me or what I do. But John Milken was being over the top right now and totally inappropriate considering what has happened to a member of his staff, and I was in no mood to just take his comments without responding.

"Wait a minute, John. This is totally inappropriate of you, and I do not appreciate your tone, your words, or your unprofessional behavior. I'm on my way there now. You and I need to sit down and discuss your issues with me at the appropriate time, but right now, we have a situation that needs our fullest attention. Don't make this worse than it already is or you will regret it," I yell, feeling the blood rushing to my head. There was simply no sense in his comments to me of which I assumed Sarah had clearly heard when he yanked the phone out of her hand.

There is a long pause, and then I hear John say to Sarah, "Here, take this. He's on his way."

Sarah then comes online and asks if I was okay and, "What was that all about?"

I say, "Don't worry, Sarah, it's been a while in coming, we'll get it settled."

She asked if there was anything she needed to do until I got there, and I told her to just keep reassuring everyone that things will be okay. I asked her if she had any update on Alice's condition, to which she responded that she had not heard anything yet, but she heard that a small group of employees followed the ambulance to the hospital. The initial responding police officer mentioned to some of our employees that the company should contact the hospital community liaison office for further information. They were also told that a police investigator would be arriving soon to talk with company officials about what happened, but she had not seen any one from the police department yet.

I know that whenever you have traumatic events happen in the work place it is very likely that some employees may not respond very well and outside consultation is required. We have a solid employee assistance program that provides for employee consultation with trained personnel to assist in overcoming their emotional concerns whenever there is such an event on the premises. I will have

Sarah reach out to our contact person at EAP and schedule either an onsite group or individual one-on-one session for each affected team member.

As I arrive to the parking lot, I see a few people standing around in small groups, obviously still in shock with what has taken place. After all, this sort of thing does not happen often and has never had here on our premises, thank God.

"Mr. McCallister, have you heard about Alice anything from the hospital?" one of the warehouse workers yells to me as I got out of my car.

"No, not yet, but I hope to get an update soon, Margarete," I yell back, recognizing the woman who inquired even if it was still pitch black at ten minutes to six.

I quickly walked over to the employees huddled in small groups to see if I could put them at ease. As I approached, they all gathered in a semicircle waiting to hear anything I might know about Alice. I told them that we don't have anything to report right now and as soon as we do, they will be the first to know because "I understand how concerned you are about Alice, but let's pray that no news right now is good news."

Another employee from the back of the crowd piped up and says, "Mr. Mac, the police officer that was here earlier asked us all of if we might know who might have shot Alice. Why would he ask us that? Do they think one of us would do this? This had to be someone who was planning to rob Alice when she went out to her car, right?"

I clear my throat and say in as calm a tome as possible, not wanting to incite any concerns whatsoever, "Well, the officer was just doing his job. That is a standard question they ask everyone on the scene when something like this happens. They have no idea when they ask it what they might learn. Let's not worry about who may have done this right now, let the police figure it out, they will get to the bottom of what happened. Please let's all take a moment of silence for Alice and wish her the best." I bow my head with the group.

Just then, my phone rings. Pulling it from my pocket, I notice it is Sam Morris, SVP of operations, John Milken's boss. Oh boy, what can this be about?

"Hi, Sam," I answer.

"Bill, what the hell is going on there?" Sam says without waiting for a response. "Do we know why Alice Randle was shot in the company parking lot last night? Who the hell would do this and for what reason? Does it have anything to do with her getting this job that you and Carl were determined for her to have? Do we know anything yet?" Sam said groggily as it was apparent he was just woken up.

I'm quite sure I know who woke him with the news. Sam was your typical high-ranking key executive who thought much more highly of himself than most everyone else in the company. He wasn't a bad guy, just full of himself when it came to having to be in on everything and anything that affected the company. He clearly saw his job and himself as the most important person at ODI next to the CEO. Most of us old-timers in the company refer to Sam as the Al Haig of ODI. For those of you who don't recall the name, Al Haig was the secretary of state under Ronald Reagan when there was an attempt to assassinate Reagan back in 1981. At that moment, Al Haig announced in a press conference following the attempt on Reagan's life that he was in charge, obviously not following the proper protocol for succession in the event a president becomes incapacitated while in office. Actually, this is not a great analogy for Sam as Mr. Haig was eventually asked to resign his position as secretary of state after several incidents of infighting and arrogance against other cabinet members. Sam is not quite that bad. He does think highly of himself though.

"Sam, I just got here, and I don't have any information about what happened or why Alice Randle was shot in the parking lot. Maybe it is related to the letter left on her doorstep, but we have no idea at this moment. The police are investigating, and I'm sure they will get to the bottom of it. I will keep you informed," I say dryly, trying to not show my irritation with his line of questioning.

"Well, do we know anything about Alice's condition yet? Which hospital was she taken to? Do you already have someone there to report back her condition?" he says in rapid-fire order.

"No, Advent Memorial, and we'll have someone on the way over there as soon as I can arrange it. Again, I just arrived here myself," I quip.

"Okay, Bill. Keep me apprised. I will be there within the hour, and let's meet with Carl as soon as possible. He'll want to be kept in the loop," he says as he hung up. Sometimes this guy drives me nuts with his arrogant attitude, but I know it's because he just cares about the company and his role. Nevertheless, I won't miss him or any of the other blowhards in this place once I walk out that door for good one day. Is that day going to ever going to get here? I find myself asking that question more and more lately, so what does that mean? Am I losing it? I hope not. Surely, the future has got to be better for me; it just has to be.

By now, that small group of night shift warehouse team members I met with dispersed, most heading home. I head inside to my office to meet with Sarah and develop a plan to deal with this new incident. Hopefully, we will soon learn about Alice's condition and it will be good news. The alternative, I hate to even consider at this point.

As I enter the outer office to my department, I see Sarah standing outside her office talking with one of the night shift warehouse supervisors. I pass them on my way to my desk and nod at both without saying a word as to not interrupt the conversation. I sit down and start to draft an action plan for discussion with Sarah so we cover all the things we need to do going forward as I know there will be many questions coming.

About a half hour later, Sarah walks in and says that she had a really interesting conversation with Tim Jernigan, the warehouse supervisor she was talking with as I came in. Sarah says that she was asking Tim if remembered anything happening while he was in the warehouse before the shooting. Tim told her that there was an argument between John and Alice earlier in the beginning of the night shift around eight o'clock.

"They were in John's office, and he heard them raising their voices to each other briefly and then Alice stormed out of the office. Shortly thereafter, Tim said John left and went home, which was the usual time he concludes his day. Alice was working the night shift and had come in around seven but that he saw her several times throughout the night and she seemed okay. Tim said he even had a meeting with her regarding an employee disciplinary matter that he needed her approval on. Otherwise, everything seemed normal just like any other work night in the warehouse.

"Then about 3:30 a.m., he heard what sounded like two small pops, almost like muffled fire cracker sounds. He said he didn't give it another thought thinking the popping sound he heard earlier was a car back firing. Then about ten minutes later, a forklift operator came running into the warehouse office where he and another supervisor were finishing up their meals and screaming that a woman who looked like Alice was lying in the parking lot on her side. They ran out to see for themselves, and that's when they found Alice lying in the parking lot covered in blood. She seemed to be alive but unconscious as they tried but could not get her to wake up or speak.

"Tim said he dialed 911 immediately while the other night supervisor went to get the security officer. He said that the first responder paramedics were there pretty quick, in about five to ten minutes, at the most. There is a fire station only two miles away. The paramedics quickly tended to Alice, but it was difficult from them to see exactly where the blood was coming from because her upper body was completely covered. Within minutes, they had her in the ambulance hooked up to several medical devices and were performing CPR. They ambulance left quickly for the hospital, and the paramedics said the police will be here shortly but do not disturb her belongings or touch anything at the scene as it appeared like she had been shot. The night security officer showed up and roped off the immediate area with packing tape. Tim said he advised the security officer to contact John Milken and HR. That's when I got the call from at home, and then I called you immediately after getting his call," Sarah said, also asking if I thought there was some connection to the shooting and the argument Tim heard between John and Alice.

"Wow, that raises an interesting question," I say pensively. "I guess we'll find out soon enough, assuming the police are aware of this."

"Tim said that he and Johnny Hendricks told the police officer everything they knew leading up to the shooting. He knows the officer wrote it all down in his report, including John's name and position with the company." Sarah then went on to say, "When I got here to the parking lot, John was already here talking with Tim and Johnny, and he seemed to be all excited about the whole situation, but he also had this strange look in his eyes. When he heard me talking to you a bit later, that's when he came over and grabbed the phone out of my hand and starting yelling at you."

"Did John say anything else to you after he gave you the phone back other than he's on his way? I did hear him say that," I ask.

"Nope, he just walked away, and I assume he went to his office and is still there as far as I know," she says with a puzzled look on her face. "You don't think he had something to do with this, do you?" Sarah asks.

"Sarah, your guess is as good as mine. I just don't know, but something doesn't seem right here. This is odd behavior even for John Milken, that's for sure."

Just about that time, Carl Johnson walks into the HR offices. "Bill, do we know anything yet? What's happening?" Carl demands as he closes the door behind him. Some of the HR staff are beginning to trickle in for the day.

"Carl, we really don't know much right now. We're trying to find out what's going on with Alice from the hospital, and we've only been able to talk with a few of the night shift team members so far. We're expecting a police investigator to be here any moment, but it's still a mystery as to exactly what happened to Alice and why," I answer, knowing he won't be satisfied with my response.

"Okay, I'll get out of your hair and let you guys do your thing. Please let me know Alice's condition immediately as soon as you hear anything. Let's plan on getting together around eleven, my office, unless you find out something sooner," he says as he turns around opens my door and walks out, disappearing around the corner as fast as he arrived.

"Whoa," says Sarah. "He was all business there, wasn't he?"

"Ah, that's Carl. A man of few words if there's nothing to discuss. We need to get busy. Do we know who from the warehouse is actually at the hospital right now and do we have a contact number?"

Sarah looks down at her note pad and says, "Yes, Deb Miller and Joe Hawkins are there. Tim gave me Deb's cell phone number."

"Okay, dial her up. Let's see if we can get through," I say urgently. Sarah dials the number using her speaker phone.

"Hello?" said the high squeaky voice on the other end.

"Hi, Deb. This is Bill McCallister from the office. I'm just checking, I understand you are there at the hospital with Alice. Can you tell us what is happening with her?"

"Oh, hi, Mr. McCallister. We don't know anything yet. She is in surgery, and they're not telling us anything yet. The nurses here said she did not look good when they brought her in, but she was still alive when they went to surgery. Oh my God, Mr. McCallister who would do this to poor Alice? She's such a good person, and she has those two young kids and no husband. We don't even know who to call," Deb says, her voice trailing off.

I glance at my list of things to do and look back to Sarah. She nods and gets up to go search the employee profiles to find out who Alice has listed as her next of kin. That's how we work—all Sarah needs is a look from me sometimes it's as if she can read my mind. Damn, that girl is good. I turn back to the phone.

"Deb, please keep me posted, will you? Call me back on this number the instant you have anything to report on Alice, anything at all. We're looking up her next of kin right now. Thank you so much, Deb!"

"Yes, sir, Mr. McCallister. I will let you know the moment I know anything."

Sarah comes back into my office and says it looks like she has listed an out-of-town relative as next of kin, a sister who lives in Marksville. "Here's her number," Sarah states and hands me a small piece of paper with the name Judy McKenzie. I dial up the number and after several rings a generic voice mail comes requesting the caller to leave a number at the beep. I leave my cell phone number with a message of immediate urgency regarding her sister. Hopefully, Ms. McKenzie will return the call soon preferably before we learn about Alice's status, especially if it happens to not be good news. Otherwise, we continue to hope for the best.

Sarah leaves to handle some "other fire" that has crossed her desk. Obviously, life goes on in the world of employee relations even as we deal with this tragic event. I find myself trying to make sense of all this and wondering if we might have a potential killer working among us here at ODI and then it dawns on me, certainly this is going through Carl Johnson's head as well. Could other team members be in danger in the future as well or was Alice the only target for this lunatic? Just as I begin to mull over the information we have so far, suddenly a very uncomfortable thought enters my head. What if this is just a random event, and Alice was a victim of outside criminal activity having nothing to do with her job? This did occur in our parking lot and could have been done by anyone as the employee parking area is easily accessible from the street. Wait a minute! WE HAVE CAMERAS out there!

"SARAH! COME HERE!" I yell from my office, as I pick up the phone and dial the security office.

Sarah comes running in with a startled look. "What happened?" she asks excitedly.

Just then, Marcus, our daytime security officer answers the phone. "Yes, Mr. McCallister, how can I help you?" He has caller ID and knew immediately I was the caller.

"Marcus, don't we have outside cameras overlooking the employee parking lot? Are they operational?" I say with urgency.

"Well, we do have cameras out there, sir, but the system has been down since last week due to a glitch in our camera monitoring relay. I'm sorry, but Mr. Milken already asked about this earlier because of what happened to Alice. Do we know anything about how she is doing, sir?" he says.

"DAMN, unbelievable!" I shout into the phone. "Uh, sorry, Marcus. I apologize. No, we don't have any information about Alice yet. I was hoping those cameras may be able to give us a clue as to what happened last night. You're sure none of the cameras on that side of the warehouse are functional?" I ask.

"No problem, sir," Marcus responds. "I'm sorry. The outside vendor has been working on them since Thursday, but they have said it will be more likely tomorrow before they are finished with the repair."

"Thank you, Marcus," I hang up the phone and look at Sarah.

"False alarm, Sarah. I was hoping the parking lot cameras were operational last night, but of course, they've been out of service since last Thursday," I say dejectedly. "I thought I had something that could help us learn who might have done this to Alice."

Sarah gave me that look of being involved in a matter of urgency, so she just turned and walked out of my office leaving me to my thoughts. Once again, a clear example of our nonverbal communication skills at work. Damn, that girl is good. I don't know what I'd do without her.

Back to reality, I've got to collect my thoughts before we have any further incidents. Besides, I have to meet with Carl in an hour, and he will be expecting a plan of action. Wow, this does complicate matters for sure. We just don't know what we don't know right now and how convenient that the cameras were incapacitated since last Thursday. Hmmm, I wonder how many people in the warehouse had knowledge of this before last night?

My cell phone rings, and I see my wife's picture pop up. "Hi, sweetie," I answer.

"Hey, babe," she says. "Thought I'd check in. Everything okay? Can you talk now?"

I hear the serious concern in her voice. "No, I don't have much information right now. Apparently, she's in surgery, but still alive, which is a great sign. I have to go. I'm sorry, but I need to prepare some things for Carl, and I'm waiting for the police to get here. Call you soon as I can, love you."

I hang up the phone as I hear her say, "No problem. Love you too!"

Just then Rosie, our HR receptionist appears at my door saying that there is a police officer at the front who would like to speak with me as soon as possible. I tell her to please bring him back, immediately. Great, now the cops are finally here. This ought to be interesting.

Much to my genuine surprise, Rosie escorts a young black man I would never suspect of being a police officer at all, not in a million years. He is tall, lanky, and extremely fragile-looking. Not someone you would ever expect as a police investigator, but you might think was more of a computer nerd.

"Good morning, sir, I'm Detective Dale Higgins from the Metro Police Department here to investigate the apparent shooting that occurred on your property last evening," he says as he flashes his blue-and-gold police badge with the words INVESTIGATOR across the top and DETECTIVE along the bottom.

"Yes, Mr. Higgins. I'm Bill McAllister, HR director. Please come in, have a seat. Can we get you something to drink? Coffee, water, soda?" I say, still not convinced this kid is a real police detective. Gee, he can't be more than twenty-five years old, and he's gotta be fresh out of the academy. How the hell could he have reached detective grade this quickly?

He declines my offer for something to drink but thanks me anyway. "Mr. McCallister, I'm here to gather as much information as possible on the shooting incident and victim, who I understand worked for your organization. Our mobile crime lab should be here shortly. I appreciate your staff cordoning off the area of the crime. I have replaced the packing tape with official crime scene tape to discourage anyone from contaminating the area. Now, I have reviewed the notes from the initial report from last night, and I will need to talk with all parties listed within who may still on the premises today and then obtain the contact information of those who have already left for the day," he says as he hands me a lengthy list of employee names. "And, by the way, anyone else that can possibly shed light on the event," he states emphatically.

Okay, so he sounds official, I'll give him that, but just call me skeptical, I still have to ask about his credentials. So I delicately respond, "Sure, of course, we have every intention of cooperating with the police on this matter. We are just as perplexed as you why this happened, and we want to get to the bottom of it as soon as possible too. However, before we proceed any further, I'd like to ask you a personal question, and I don't mean any disrespect at all, but you seem to awful young to be a detective with the Metro Police. If you don't mind me asking, how much experience do you have as a detective?"

"Yes," he slowly drawls. "I'm sure I am not what you were expecting, Mr. McCallister, and I can see you might be concerned about my capabilities, but let me assure you I am every bit qualified and certified as a homicide investigator under the state statutes. My full name is Dale Higgins, and I graduated from the police academy at the top of my class two years ago. I served one year as a patrol officer and then another year working with our senior detective in charge of the department, learning the procedures and accompanying him on many separate investigations. I assisted in investigating seventeen felony cases and the apprehension of thirty-two individuals resulting in convictions on all but four of those charged with the crimes. I think I have proven myself and our chief of police awarded me the title of Detective Investigator last month. This is my third individual case since my promotion, and I am committed to doing the best job possible, and your case will be no different. I hope you will soon feel that I am well-qualified to handle this case and bring whoever is responsible for the crime to justice. I will make it a personal priority to resolve this matter as expeditiously as possible and with minimal disruption to your operations. Can I count on your full support, sir?"

Okay well, I've been around a pretty long time, and I have had the wool pulled over my eyes in the past, but not lately over the last ten to fifteen years—none that I'm willing to admit to anyway. Reluctantly, my initial instincts on Mr. Dale Higgins were all wrong right from the beginning, but I'm thoroughly impressed with his cool demeanor and quiet confidence. So much so that I don't have a good reason to suspect he won't give his full attention to this matter. Then again, do I really have any choice here?

"Of course, Investigator Higgins. I sincerely apologize if I offended you in anyway, I meant no disrespect. You will have our full support, and anything we can do to help the Metro Police solve this crime, please rely on us for cooperation," I say without hesitation.

"Okay, sir. Thank you," he says. "Why don't we get down to work?"

Investigator Higgins and I spent the next hour going over his list of employee contacts, discussing Alice Randle and her employment record here at ODI. He wanted as much information as I would reveal about Alice and her relationships with other team members. At first, I was a little reluctant to share all the events surrounding her promotion to assistant GM in the warehouse, but after he quickly picked up that she had been promoted above other qualified male candidates for the position, I had no choice but to share the note left on Alice's door step. I buzzed Sarah to step in and bring the note Alice had given us on Monday. Within a few minutes, Sarah popped in and handed me the note.

As I was passing it over to Detective Higgins, I couldn't help but notice his eyes were fixated on Sarah as if he had never seen a female before. Now, Sarah is not only an intelligent woman, she is also very presentable and makes a very good appearance. But I never really thought of her as attractive; probably because she is very efficient and extremely dedicated. Besides, she has a plan for her life, and she is determined to reach her goals which is why I'm sure she has never presented herself otherwise.

"Oh, Sarah, this is Detective Higgins from the Metro Police," I say as he stands up, dropping his notepad on the floor. While he bends down to pick up the notepad, I wait for him to stand before saying, "Detective Higgins, Sarah Jenkins, our employee relations manager. Sarah had spoken with Alice on Monday when she was in here to tell us about the note and threatening voice mails, she had received."

Officer Higgins offered his hand to Sarah, and she responded with, "Good to meet you," as she shook his hand. I couldn't help but see that their handshake seemed a bit longer than normal. It wasn't difficult to understand that Detective Higgins might be a bit smitten by Sarah. Although I wasn't certain Sarah had the same feeling about him, at least at this point anyway.

I asked Sarah to go over the events of Monday when Alice was waiting for her when she arrived at work. Sarah began her recollection of the conversation with Alice for Detective Higgins, and it was pretty clear he had several more questions than I thought necessary which I suspect was his way of keeping Sarah talking. Perhaps it was just his way of interviewing for information. After all, he was a police detective and asking questions is how he operates. Hmm... just seemed like there was a little more to his line of questioning for Sarah than just obtaining the facts.

When he had run out of questions, Sarah asked if she could be excused to go catch up on some other things that were pending. I turned to Detective Higgins and asked, "Is that all we need with Sarah?"

He cleared his throat and said, "Sure, yeah. I think I have enough for now. But please allow me to reconnect with you if I have other questions arise in the future, Sarah. It was very nice to meet you!"

"Same here," Sarah said, getting up and reaching for the door. I couldn't swear by it, but I thought I heard a big sigh as she left my office.

Based on all the information Sarah shared, Higgins added all of the other supervisors who were not on duty last night to the list of those he wanted to speak with. Of course, the hierarchy of management throughout the company were of interest to his investigation and many of them made the hit list as well. Okay, so it looks like he will be talking with more than fifty team members, including management—quite a large task for sure.

We finally ended our conversation after two long hours before walking outside to the employee parking lot. He immediately spotted the camera placements and inquired about how they work and the possibility of getting the recordings. When I informed him that they were currently under repair and not working since last Thursday, he made a quick note to his pad. I did not ask or probe to learn if he had the same question I had been thinking earlier about who might have had knowledge of this before last night. But after spending the last hour with him, I felt like we were on the same planet in many ways. Yes, sir, I was completely convinced Investigator Higgins would do a thorough job of investigating this matter, which would hopefully result in finding out who did this terrible thing to Alice, one of ODI's employees. Even though her promotion to the second-in-command in the warehouse has been an exercise of disruption for my department, to say the least. This was a human being, and no matter what, she did not deserve this at all, nope. No one should ever regret a promotion to better their lot in life. It's the American dream—start at the bottom and work your way up. That's what most of us strive for when we enter the workforce to make a living and provide for our families. I couldn't help but wonder what this might do to our recruiting efforts going forward.

However, my thoughts were abruptly interrupted by Investigator Higgins's voice. What I did not expect at this point was his comment that this was now a homicide investigation, and any further information that I became aware of going forward should be treated as confidential and only shared with him.

"Wait! What? A HOMICIDE INVESTIGATION? So Alice Randle is dead? How do you know this?" I said in complete shock. I was never out of his presence for the past hour, and he did not receive a call, how could he know this?

"Mr. McCallister, the moment Alice Randle arrived at the hospital, we already had a police officer there for her protection and with hopes of obtaining information in the event she may have regained consciousness. Unfortunately, I received a text that she did not survive her wounds and was pronounced dead at 9:22 a.m. from two separate gun shots, one to the upper torso piercing the left lung cavity and the other, probably the most fatal, a shot to the forehead just above the left eye. I'm so sorry to inform you of this, but obviously we have a lot of work to do, and I must insist on your complete confidentiality, sir."

I was dumbfounded, I could not even speak, so I have no idea how the words came out of my mouth, but I heard my voice, "Yes, of course, I understand."

"Also, Mr. McCallister, if you receive a call from Ms. Randle's sister, please refer her to call the contact number I gave you earlier, my cell phone. I think it would be best for the Metro Police to inform her of this incident and the status. Besides, I think your attorney may want to advise your management staff of what information you should release to the public, your employees, or any relative connected to Ms. Randle. In a homicide case, what happens in the first few days can set the direction and potentially affect the outcome of a case, including accountability. I will be in touch as soon as I have further information or I need to obtain or clarify details as we go forth. Do you have any questions for me at this time?"

Investigator Higgins turned and left me to walk over to the mobile crime lab trailer. Still reeling from the terrible news, my mind was going a million miles a second trying to make sense of everything. Little did I know that this was just the beginning of things to come. Right now, I needed to call CeCe, I just needed to hear her calming voice. She was always good about settling me down when I had something was bothering me. She has always been a great sounding board for things like watching someone's emotional breakdown while sitting in on their termination or resolving a dispute between a manager and an upset team member, which could go any number of different ways. However, this was way beyond those seemingly insignificant events right now. I was just hoping my loving wife could work her magic on me, as my hands were shaking like an old man with Parkinson's disease. What I really needed right now was a drink, a smooth bourbon would do me just fine, but that was not possible right now. Damn! Not yet, but I can certainly see that in my immediate future.

I speed dial CeCe and instantly get her voice recording, which tells me she is on the phone. I leave her a very short message, "911, ASAP," was our code for "Call immediately, we need to talk." Thankfully, it has been seldom used since we put it in place several years ago.

As soon as I hit the disconnect on my phone, it rings and without looking, thinking it was CeCe, I say, "Hi, hun. Listen, I know you're busy but I really need to talk."

"Why, Mr. McCallister, I didn't realize you thought so highly of me," said the female voice on the other end.

"Uh, what? Oh, you're not CeCe. Sorry, I was expecting a call from my wife," I mumbled sheepishly. It was Jayne Davis calling.

"Well, I'm still flattered, but speaking of expectation, Mr. Johnson was expecting you at 11:00 a.m., may I tell him you are on your way, sir?" Jayne said in her usually professional way.

"Oh yes, Jayne, thank you. I'm on my way right now." Great… looking at my watch, 11:15. I lost track of time dealing with the police investigator. Oh well, Johnson will understand, I hope. I have no any idea how he'll react when I announce the news about Alice. As I hurry back into the building, my phone goes off again, it's CeCe returning my call. I guess support will have to be put on hold for right now.

"Hi, babe, thanks for calling back. Bad news, Alice Randal has passed away from her injuries, but I need to call you back. I'm on my way to see Carl, he doesn't even know yet."

I hear a muffled gasp on the other end. "Oh, Bill. I'm so sorry. Yes, please call me when you can.," she says and hangs up.

As I walk through the outer office where Jayne sits, I notice she is on the phone and I hear her comment about making arrangements to send flowers to the family. What? Does Carl already know about Alice? how could he? I just found out not five minutes ago from the primary source. Wow, bad news travels fast. As I push open the door to Carl's office, I see Sam Morris and John Milken seated in front of Carl's desk talking low, almost whispering and leaning toward each other as if they did not want anyone to hear their conversation, while Carl is on the phone. Hmmm, maybe they were just trying not to bother Carl. But as soon as they both saw me walk in, they immediately stopped their conversation and straightened back up in their seats.

"Good morning, Bill," Sam says under his breath. John just looks away and then nods when I take an open seat beside them facing Carl.

I responded, "Morning, gentlemen. Hope your day has been better than mine." I almost wish I had not said it that way, but it was out there and too late to take it back.

"Okay, Bill. What's going on?" Sam says in a very inquisitive way.

"Oh, well, I need to give Carl and you guys an update on Alice, but I'll wait until he gets off the phone."

"Well, he might be a while Bill. He's trying to get a status on Alice now, but if you already know something, let's hear it," Sam replies.

Just in the nick of time, Carl hangs up and says, "No go on getting any information from the hospital officials, patient-doctor only rules. They're trying to reach her next of kin which I guess we're trying to do as well, huh, Bill?"

I nod swallowing hard, "Well, I just heard from the investigating officer. Unfortunately, Alice Randall did not survive the gunshot wounds and surgery to save her life. He was notified by text from another officer at the hospital monitoring her progress hoping to get information, if and when she regained consciousness. This is now an official homicide investigation."

There was a moment or two of complete silence until Carl said, "Okay, gentlemen, this is now out of our hands, and we need to be fully transparent and cooperating completely with the Metro Police, and that goes for everyone in the company. In addition, if this turns out to be an internal issue, then we'll need to be ready to act swiftly to settle the employee base as obviously this will not be viewed well for ODI. I think we need to get our marketing communications people together to start developing a company response for both internal and external purposes. Bill, you and Sam will need to clear your calendars for the next few days as we're going to be inundated with news reporters soon, I'm sure of it."

The statements Carl made were right on target. He is thinking of the big-picture impact, but I also know there will a huge number of unanswered questions from our team members. A significant plan of action will be necessary if ODI is to get through this unscathed with minimal impact to productivity. Right now, we have a more pressing task in front of us. How do we announce the murder of a fellow employee right here on our premises in the most delicate way so as to not alarm the workforce and set off a series of other employee issues as a result? Well, my work week just got even more complicated. Can things get any worse? Little did I know at that moment, the level of worse is only in the mind of what you know, not what you think.

Carl, Sam, and I agree to reconvene with the marketing communications director and her assistant as soon as Jayne can get us all scheduled in the main conference room. Carl is all about company image and how ODI is ultimately viewed to the outside, but I also know he wants to do what's best for our team members, and I could sense his concern for them as news gets about Alice.

I walk back to my office somewhat still in shock from the morning's events. When I drove into the office yesterday, a little more than twenty-four hours ago, as usual I had no idea what I might expect from work this week. I certainly did not anticipate having to deal with a murder right here on our premises. This is way more than usual and customary even for me. Man, I'd give anything to have that bourbon right now! And I don't even care if someone might think I could be a borderline alcoholic with thoughts such as this. I'm just thinking it would be nice; of course, I won't ever act on it. No, not in a million years...well, maybe a million years is too long, but I'm sure I would not ever drink on the job. Nope, I've had to deal with team members in that capacity before, and I don't ever see myself doing that. Well, uh, not up until today anyway. Hell, that drink does sound pretty good right now, I don't care what you say; I'm only human.

I walk into the outer office to HR and motion for Sarah to join me in my office. I need to tell her about Alice as gently as possible, which I don't relish doing, but she needs to know right way. Sarah comes in and closes the door behind her.

"I have news about Alice's sister. She called my phone while you were outside with the investigator. She's on her way here as we speak and should be arriving late today," she says, looking at me inquisitively expecting to hear my news.

"Um, well, uh… Have a seat, Sarah, please. I don't know any other way to say this but just to let you know that Alice has passed away. She didn't survive the surgery," I said solemnly.

Sarah let out a big sigh and said, "I kind of expected that, sir. After hearing that she had been shot twice, I kind of thought it would be unlikely if she survived. I've seen gunshot victims before growing up, and usually, if they have more than just one, then they generally don't survive," she said in a matter-of-fact way.

Instantly, I was reminded of the difficult life Sarah has had to endure in the past.

"Yes, I was hoping for the best, but nonetheless, it's just a tragic event that we need to deal with and eventually help our team members at ODI get past. Carl, Sam, and I are going to meet with Sheila Smith from marketing and her team to develop a plan of action in response to our employees and the outside going forward. I'd like you to be there as well. As the employee relations manager, I think your insight will be helpful to this effort."

"Of course," Sarah says. "But let me ask you, sir. Who do you think might have done this? I mean, it just seems strange that there has been all this talk about Alice and John Milken being together, she gets promoted, and then she receives threatening voice mails and a letter left on her doorstep to shame her into quitting. She comes to HR to report the threats and then she is gunned down in the employee parking lot, here at work. Doesn't make a lot of sense that someone who was passed over for a job promotion would take it that far. Just seems to me we might be missing something," she says suspiciously.

"Okay. Sarah, what are you saying? Apparently, you have some idea of who may responsible for doing all this? Who?" I ask.

"Well, I don't really know but what if the threats about her job don't have anything to do with her being shot but are connected in another way?" Sarah says.

"Okay, Sarah, just spit it out. I'm not following you. Do you know something that I don't?" I say with a genuine blank look on my face.

"Well," she goes on. "It's just something Judy McKenzie, Alice's sister, said to me on the phone when she returned your call after I told her about Alice. She then asked if we had notified John. When I asked her who she was referring to, she replied that he was a warehouse manager. I told her that yes, John was well-aware and was already on the premises. Now, I didn't give that any more thought at the time since she might have been just making sure that Alice's boss knew about what had happened. Then I remembered that Tim had told me he had heard Alice and John Milken arguing in his office before John had left for the day yesterday."

"And so you think John Milken has something to do with this, is that it?" I said suspiciously.

"I'm not saying that directly but how and why does Alice's sister know who John is or at least his name, hmm?" Sarah quips.

"Okay, Sarah, I see where you're going. Okay, John Milken is not a pillar of society, and yes, he is a very gruff and rough person, being an ex-Army guy. And I know he is not a friend of HR, especially not of mine anyway." I chuckle.

"But why would he try to discredit her with threatening voice mails, leaving a nasty note on her doorstep, and then is somehow involved in shooting her in the parking lot? I just don't see the connection, if he really wanted her out of the job all he would need to do was come up with some performance issues, blaming her for incompetence and that would be more likely John's MO, don't you think?" I retorted.

"Besides, he has an argument with her in his office before he leaves for the day and then returns later that night and shoots her? Doesn't add up to me, Sarah. Um, maybe you just need to share your concerns with Inspector Higgins, and he can look into it. I'm just not sure," I say with a lot of skepticism.

About that time, my phone rings and I see it is CeCe. Sarah excuses herself and leaves my office.

"Hi, sweetie, thanks for calling. It's been a wild day, and I'm so tired already. I look forward to getting out of here and getting home to you."

I spent the next several minutes bringing my wife up to speed on what has happened, what we know—which isn't much—and making plans going forward. As usual, she gives me tremendous moral support just from the tone in her voice, and I am reminded how lucky I am to have this wonderful woman in my life. I don't know what I would do without her. I have a feeling that the drink of bourbon would become a bottle of bourbon, and I would then qualify to be a full-blown alcoholic, for sure!

Later that afternoon, Carl, Sam, Sarah, and I met with Sheila Smith, the director of marketing and her communications manager, Sally Henshaw, to discuss the communication effort ODI would put together to our team members.

Sheila was a portly, tall woman who was all about first impressions. She began working for ODI as marketing rep four years ago, and I recall having to intervene between her and another coworker a few weeks after she started regarding an argument about appropriate dress for the office. Sheila was always dressed to the tee—ultra-business attire, complete with the phony greeting and fake smile. She had chastised another rep regarding her choice of clothes. The marketing director at that time was very nonconfrontational so the disagreement continued throughout the day, escalating to a full-blown argument which could be heard throughout the floor. Of course, the director called HR for someone to come and rescue him from having to settle the matter in his own department. I happened to be the lucky one to respond as my staff had already left for the day. While the argument was settled pretty quickly, I was sure this would issue would rear its ugly head again, sometime down the road. As it turned out, Sheila's coworkers learned pretty quickly that it wasn't a hill to die on, so it never became an issue with them going forward.

However, I recall the first time I crossed swords with Sheila after she had ascended to the role of director for the marketing department. Being overly focused on setting and maintaining the corporate image, she routinely doled out harsh discipline for her team members who did not reflect that image at all times. To her credit, they never crossed that line going forward, but I had begun planting the seeds on getting our senior-level executives to understand the changing workplace environment. With the new challenges of recruiting and more millennial-age applicants coming into the workplace, it was not easy enforcing stringent dress code policies that were becoming less mainstream to these candidates as time passed. Our senior staff, being more old-school in their thinking and seeking to have a department of employees who looked like themselves, just didn't work in today's world. Especially these new young adults were getting tattoos and piercings in greater numbers as it was becoming more accepted in society, and the workplace was no different. I felt that it was up to me to try and educate our leaders on what we faced on the recruiting front, and if we were going to be a destination of choice for these highly talented applicants, we would need to be open to change.

Since Sheila was hell-bent on having a standard dress code policy, which included hiring only clean-cut, with no visible tattoos or piercings, she objected to any attempt I made to broach the subject at our staff meetings. She was adamant in stating her case, and without bringing any ammunition to the table, our conversations about work ethic and employees' appearance went absolutely nowhere. She just could not bring herself to accept anything she considered less than her opinion.

So I decided to approach the matter from a different angle. I asked her to join me for lunch at the mall food court, which I normally avoid at all cost. Finally, she reluctantly accepted after declining my invitation for almost two months before agreeing to meet there. I'm sure she was expecting me to try and befriend her just to get her on my side in the staff meeting conversations to relax our archaic dress code policy, which she had so proudly served on the committee to draft several years ago. But that was not my plan, no, sir...not at all.

As it turned out, there was an Italian food place in the mall that had surprisingly decent grub, for a hole-in-the-wall mall eatery. We met there around noon, and after ordering our food and picking up our food trays, we found a quite table off to the side from the main seating area.

"Okay, Bill," Sheila started, "You didn't ask me to join you for lunch here because the cuisine is something to die for. I know you want me to reconsider my stand on hiring marketing staff who do not meet our current written guidelines, which have been in place for some time, I might add. I truly believe that making a good impression the first time with clients is very important. To me, that goes a long way in getting a business commitment and getting business is what my department is all about." Her determination was resolute.

"Look, Sheila, I don't disagree with your position at all, and I do understand why expect your team members to be shining stars because you folks represent the face of the company. While that is vitally important, I get it, no argument here. But I think a blanket dress code policy cannot be the standard for all employee positions. I need you to you know the tremendous obstacle my recruiting team has trying to source candidates that only meet stringent appearance criteria for positions that do not have outside client contact."

"But, Bill," Sheila protested, "if we don't have a consistent program for physical appearance for a team member who joins our company, how can I seriously consider them for a higher-level opening down the road that does require that they meet with outside clients?"

"Okay, I agree that it can be an issue, but maybe not," I said as she looked at me inquisitively. "Physical appearance is not a defendable qualification by virtue of the EEOC, the Equal Employment Opportunity Commission. We are allowed to have specific job qualifications that are necessary to perform the duties of the position. These are referred to as BFOQs or Bonafide Occupational Qualifications. However, unless we can defend each qualification on its own merit, then we run the risk of systematic discrimination. And we will be a prime target for attorneys just looking to capitalize on those disgruntled applicants and team members who did not get a job because of their appearance. There are several court cases that support this as a growing trend in employment law." I pause for a moment to let her ask any other questions.

While she was taking this in, I asked her to look around. "What do you see? Who do you see working at the food court businesses?"

Slowly, she scanned the different options for a getting food, and when her gaze returned to me, I said, "How many of those working in here do you see that have tattoos? Their hairstyle in a different color? Or with some kind of facial hair? Do you understand why they work at these businesses here in the mall? If not, these businesses could not hire or keep enough staff if they had strict dress code policies."

"But, Bill," she argued, "they aren't the kind of candidate we would even interview at ODI. They would not be qualified to do the work, certainly not in my department!"

"Precisely," I said. "And by law, we can require that anyone that applies for a specific position with ODI have a minimum skill set of qualifications, or we do not have to consider them for employment, but physical appearance is not a skill set. Can we decide to hire based on who we feel is best qualified? Yes, of course, and if you have two or more candidates equally qualified for a job, you should have no problem hiring any one of them as long as they meet the legal job requirements we establish. We just can't legally have a written quali-fication that eliminates candidates based on their appearance."

"Okay, I get your point," she said. "That's why you're the HR expert; you keep us out of trouble," she says, laughing as she shakes her head and finishes her salad.

With Sheila's expertise, we draft a press release for the news media who were already trying to get a statement from ODI on the murder of an employee last night. We do not give out any specific information except to announce that an investigation into the matter was being conducted by the Metro Police. Obviously, we knew that it would not be enough so a contingency plan is developed that Sally would relay to the press as the inquires came forth. It isn't long, and the hounds were at the door, not thirty minutes after we sent the initial press release in to the news outlets.

Just as I start to pack up for the day, I glance at the clock on the wall, 5:30. Well, I've been here just about an entire twelve hours, and I feel every minute of it. My desk phone rings, and I hear a voice asking to speak with Bill McCallister. I tell the caller I am he and, "What can I do for you?"

It's Investigator Higgins and he would like to establish a meeting with John Milken tomorrow and would like for me to be a part of it. I tell him that was no problem, just let me know when he will be available, and I'll have it set up. He also asks about getting the names of any the next of kin for Alice. I mention that we have notified her sister who is driving down from Marksville later today. We hope to meet with her in the morning. Higgins thinks it might be better if he is also present at that meeting in hopes he can learn something that might shed light on the case. But I start to feel a bit uncomfortable with someone from the police department asking to be a part of conversations with other ODI personnel so I tell him I will get back to him. He asks me what concern I might have with his request. I'm wondering about the possibility of compromising the confidentiality of his investigation. Is it appropriate for him to question ODI employees in my presence? I wasn't sure about that. He made it very clear that none of the employees he would be talking with are obligated to say anything, but if they are open to talking, he feels like it could be helpful to the investigation. Interrogations of key witnesses and potential suspects will be done later at police headquarters after getting some basic information from those who might have known Alice best. Okay, then, who am I to say no to the police? It's his investigation, and he should know if what he's requesting might compromise his investigation or not. He asks if someone could leave a message on his phone for the meeting times with John Milken and Alice's sister. I mention this to Sarah as I pass by her office to say goodnight. She informs me that Judy McKenzie is supposed to call first thing in the morning. I ask her to try to get that meeting set for 10:00 a.m., and I will call John to see when he can meet Investigator Higgins and myself. That should be fun...hmm, not sure how he will take it with me there while Higgins asks his questions. But, hey, I didn't ask to be there; I was requested to be there. John still won't believe that. I tell Sarah that she needs to get out of here and go home; she's done quite enough today already. She laughs and then assures me that she will be leaving shortly.

It has been a very long day, and as I point the car in the direction of home, I don't even care what time it is, I will be having that Four Roses and losing myself in some smooth jazz. And if anyone tries to stop me, well, let's just say a man on a mission is not someone you want to mess with! A thousand thoughts are going through my mind as I reflect on the events of the day. Waking up to a call in the wee hours, a shooting at my place of work, understandably anxious team members, a police investigation, and then the untimely death of a woman in the middle of it all. But I keep coming back to the conversation I had with Sarah...Have I missed something? She is really good at analyzing a situation where someone isn't being completely forthright; she's a lot better at that than I ever was, even at my best. She seems to be convinced that in some way, somehow, John Milken is involved with this more than appears to be evident. Sarah will share her thoughts with Investigator Higgins tomorrow. Guess we'll see if he thinks there's any merit to her suspicions. Even if it turns out there's no connection with John at all, I can't help feeling a bit elated at knowing he could be on the hot seat as I suspect Higgins is quite the formidable police interrogator. He may be wiry-looking and appear more suited to be sitting behind a monitor, banging out code on a keyboard, but I have a feeling he has a dark side, a very dark side that probably displays itself when he has a suspect in his sights. Seventeen felony cases and twenty-eight convictions all in the last year! Oorah! I don't think old John Milken knows just what he's in for! Yep, I can't help but smile about that. Man, that bourbon is gonna taste a bit sweeter and smoother tonight, that's for sure!

After not having the best night's sleep, I'm up early the next morning, way before the alarm. I'm anticipating a really busy and critical day for Ocean Direct Inc. CeCe instinctively senses my anxiety and asks if there's anything she can do after hearing details of yesterday's events. As I gather my things to leave I try to minimize her concerns, "Well, I guess we'll see what the day brings. But I'm sure this is a random act of violence, and Alice was just in the wrong place at the wrong time."

She gives me a tight hug and whispers in my ear in a sultry sexy way that when I get a chance, I should call my lover. Now, right there, for a split second, I totally forgot about ODI, Alice Randle, and what has happened. That woman can flip me like a light switch, and she knows it—and I relish it every time she does! While I suspect my day will be filled with a lot more than just the usual employee issues, I know that life away from my job is a true sanctuary for me, and CeCe is the major contributor. In a way, I know I will miss the antics of employee behavior and the weird, strange things team members do when their emotional reactions are out of control. But after so many years, I think I've had more than my fair share of dealing with this craziness. Yep, it's time for someone else to step in and take over. Maybe someone else will be able to anticipate human behavior better than I have…but I don't really believe that at all.

The commute into work is uneventful, and I actually arrive in good time. Occasionally, you hit the traffic and stop lights just right, almost like the commuting gods throw you a bone every now and then just to break your balls over the next ten trips; their way of keeping you from building up any mental resistance to the norm.

I open the outer door and walk toward the hallway leading to my department passing several of the office staff who work for various department leaders. Even with their half smiles and obligatory "good mornings," I sense a strange look in their eyes. By now, the word has spread throughout the company about the shocking events of yesterday and that we lost a member of our family in such a horrific way. It then occurs to me that while most know my role will concern the investigation for this event, as the HR Director, I will also be expected to help team members come to terms with this tragedy. People tend to internalize tragic events when they happen to others even more so if they don't make any sense. In due time, everyone will need to put this somewhere within the recess of their mind in order to carry on, but all in due time. The death of someone you work with or just barely know ranks right up there with losing a loved one as far as impact on the human spirit. The Swiss psychiatrist Elisabeth Kubler-Ross developed a theory describing the stages of human emotion one might experience when facing the loss of a loved one or our own terminal illness. The Five Stages of Grief, as she labeled them include: denial, anger, bargaining, depression, and acceptance. She concluded that in order to return to anywhere near close to normal after a tragic event occurs, we must recognize where the afflicted individual is on the spectrum; not everyone will go through each stage and there is no specific time frame where each person will be. As a responsive HR function dealing with human emotion in the workplace, it is essential that we have tools at our disposal to help team members deal with this type of tragic event. People are just people—you never know what to expect, so you need to be prepared for just about anything.

As I settle in and get my desktop computer up to speed, I remember that I need to find out when John Milken can meet today so I pick up the phone and dial his extension.

"Hello, what do you need, Bill?" says the gruff voice on the other end.

"Well, good morning to you too, John. Listen, the police investigator assigned to looking into the case with Alice would like to talk with you sometime today. When is a good time for you?" I say, telling more than asking.

"What?" John cries. "Who and what the hell does he want with me?" he says indignantly.

"John," I say slowly, "the police are investigating what happened to Alice and they want to—"

"Hold up, McCallister," John interrupts. "Why does he want to talk with me? Does he think I had something to do with it?"

"Look, John, I'm the messenger here. He's talking to everyone and anyone who worked with Alice. Come on, did you really think they're weren't going to want to talk with you? She was your direct report for Christ's sake!" I say.

There was a long pause before John says, "Okay, might as well get this over with. When will they be here?"

"John, the investigator will be here this morning, but he needs to review some information from the files first. How about later this afternoon? Maybe around three o'clock?" I offer, smiling inside, thinking a delay will make him sweat some!

"Uh, no. Let's do this first thing this afternoon. I'm leaving early today," John mutters.

"Okay, we'll make 1:00 p.m. and we'll meet in the HR conference room," I say as I hang up the phone, not wanting to give him any chance to object. *Jerk*, I think to myself. *Why is he so worried about talking to the police? Especially if he doesn't have anything to hide. Hmm...maybe he's just being John, obstinate and uncooperative as usual.*

I dial Higgins's number to leave a message, but he picks up the call anyway. He will be here around 10:00 a.m. to meet with Judy McKenzie and stay over until the one o'clock with Milken. He mentions that he would like to also see John Milken's personnel file. Normally, I would not allow anyone from the outside other than a team member to view their personnel file, but in this case, Higgins will probably have the district attorney subpoena it anyway, why then delay the inevitable? So there you go, my whole day looks to be planned out already, and I haven't even had that delicious first cup of cheap aged office coffee that I so treasure! I even amuse myself sometimes!

I get busy going through my emails, which I've badly neglected so far this week. I usually stay on top of email as I'm not crazy about having to read and respond anyway, but I learned long ago that if I keep it caught up every day, then it's not so bad. But now I have a legitimate excuse, but not one that I am cherishing by the way.

Before I get too far down the list of several hundred, Rosie buzzes me.

"Hi, Rosie. How are you this morning?" I ask.

"Good morning, sir. I am doing just great. Boy, you are here early?" she says.

"Yes, I knew this was going to be a busy day," I say as I inform her about the meetings on my calendar and ask that she make sure we have fresh coffee and water available.

"Yes, sir, no problem. I will take care of that," she replies and hangs up with her customary, "Have a nice day!"

Looking at my watch, I see I have about two hours before the ten o'clock with Higgins and Alice's sister. Good, that should give me time to catch up these emails, provided I get no more interruptions. For the next two hours, I work diligently at removing emails, responding to those important and deleting those that are not. Just then my phone rings and I see from the caller ID it's my friend Charlie.

"Morning, Charlie. What's going on in your world?"

"Hey, buddy, how you doing? What's all this about somebody getting killed down there at your work? It's all over the news this morning," he says inquisitively.

"It's tragic, Charlie. We had a night manager shot and killed Monday night," I responded.

"So, do you know who might've done it? You know it's usually the ex, the girlfriend or the lover or the jealous husband or wife," he announces like he's telling me something I don't already know.

"Yes, yes, Charlie. The Metro Police are investigating. They will get to the bottom of who did it, I'm sure. Look, I have to run got another call coming in, my friend," I said quickly.

"Okay, pal, catch you later. Hope to see you guys this weekend." He hangs up and I switch over to the ringing line. It's Sarah telling me that Alice McKenzie is here for our ten o'clock. She will have her waiting in the conference room until Higgins gets here and I am ready. Higgins actually arrives right on time so we all convene in the small HR conference room, designed for no more than ten, so it's plenty big enough for the four of us.

Judy is a slightly older woman than her sister was, and after introductions and hearing her voice, I strongly suspect she is a heavy smoker. That, and the fact she obviously had one or two in the parking lot before she came in the building. The aroma of cigarette smoke was thick in the room. We let Higgins conduct the meeting and ask the questions since this was more his meeting than ours anyway. We learned a lot about Alice we did not know and some of it was not good to hear. Apparently, she had been married for twelve years to an abusive husband who was also an alcoholic, and they had two children. She left the relationship only after several years of progressively worsening physical and mental abuse from her husband, culminating into a final act where he beat her so bad she had to be hospitalized for three days with severe internal injuries. We also learned that the two sisters were abandoned at an early age because their father had passed away when they were just toddlers, and their mother could not support them. She gave them up for adoption, and then later passed away at the young age of forty due to a drug overdose. Obviously, a very sad life for all involved, but it spoke volumes for why Alice aspired to make the best of her personal situation by working hard and demonstrating a strong work ethic. Now, she had been murdered just as she had climbed into the responsible role of assistant warehouse director. Clearly, a complete tragedy in the worst way.

But what we really wanted to know was about her comment she made to Sarah when informed of her sister's death that Alice was seeing a man named John who was a manager in the warehouse where she worked. That kind of narrowed it down, since John Milken is the only person in the warehouse with that first name. All she could confirm is that Alice had told her she was currently seeing a man named John, but she does not know the extent of the relationship nor his last name. However, she thinks it must be a serious relationship since Alice has never mentioned the name of anyone else. She knows Alice has been a party girl ever since she left her ex-husband. She has hooked up with several guys during that time, staying with each of them at their residence until the relationship went sour, which wasn't long at all. Judy is not able to provide any of their names since Alice has never mentioned anyone of them by name, which told her that they were not serious at all. Officer Higgins asked several more questions about Alice's lifestyle, and if Judy may know anyone else Alice was in contact with who may have an issue with her. He obtains information on the ex-husband and where Alice frequented in the past few years after her divorce. Judy is helpful in providing that information, to the best of her recollection. Obviously, this is a delicate conversation and is not treated as a formal police investigation, even though it was. I give Higgins full credit for that, since he was in total control. Judy leaves our meeting knowing she definitely has her work cut out for her, making funeral arrangements and knowing she has decisions to make regarding Alice's children, which are still elementary age and staying with the day sitter, a close friend of Alice's who has the kids overnight when Alice was at work. Little did they know that their mother would not be there when they got home from school. How sad is that? Keeps you reminded just how precious life can be.

The meeting with Judy only lasts about thirty minutes so as the three of us continue, Higgins is most interested in John Milken and his history with ODI. Sarah retrieved his personnel file, and Higgins begins reading every document in the lengthy file. After all, John has been with ODI for thirty-two years; there was a ton of documentation in his file but nothing that Higgins would find interesting, but that didn't deter him from doing his job. I am not surprised. So while he read through all the exhaustive paperwork in John's file, I excuse myself and went back to my office. I know Sarah would be there with Higgins, and I suspect they both want me to leave anyway, so I oblige. Of course, Sarah is going to share her thoughts on John Milken, which I am all in favor of. At least it won't be me throwing John under the bus with the police, but somehow, I have a strange feeling it will come back to me anyway, since Sarah was my direct report.

I really need to finish getting through those emails. God, I really hate this part of the job. Business emails have become the best and the worst of what business is all about. Yes, emails provide instant feedback and information that can certainly be extremely timely in decision-making, potentially saving or garnering an organization BUKU dollars. But the invention and use of emails for communication purposes has definitely created more work for everyone, that's for sure. I know, I'm dating myself here, but I preferred it when business communication was done in person; a lost art these days! I work feverishly to get through the emails before lunch, and I felt good that I only had a few left to go before my stomach started to growl. "FEED ME," it was telling me! It was right at noon, and I stick my head in the conference room where Higgins is sitting still going through John's file.

"You up for lunch before the one o'clock with your warehouse director?" I ask.

"Uh, no you go ahead, I'll grab something later. I really want to get through his file before one," he says without really looking up.

"Okay, be glad to bring you something," I offer.

"No, no, it's okay. Thanks anyway," he replies.

I turn and head for the door. As I climb into the car, I remember that I need to call CeCe. That remark about I should call my lover is on my mind, do you blame me? I hit the speed dial and it starts to ring.

"Hi, my lover. I was told I should give you a call when I had a chance!"

"Oh, hi there, lover man," she says in that sexy voice only she can do on occasion. "How is your day going?"

"It's moving along. That's about all I can say. It's not over by a long shot. We still have to talk to Milken this afternoon."

"Oh?" she sighs. "That's probably not going to be a box of chocolates for you, is it?"

"Well, at least I won't be asking the questions," I tell her. "The police investigator will be calling the shots. But it might get interesting anyway. When I informed John of the meeting with police, he wasn't happy, as you might imagine."

"Well, good luck, sweetie. I'm thinking about you," she says. "Hey, tonight why don't we just curl up on the couch and watch a good comedy movie on Netflix?"

"Wow! That sounds awesome, lover girl. And who knows? We might not even finish watching the whole thing this time!" I say with a little chuckle.

"Promises, promises…We'll see, tiger…but only if you will let me distract you from all this negative karma around you. I'll have your bourbon waiting!" She says the magic words, music to my ears.

I come back with, "CeCe, you're the best. You know that I love you, girl, right?"

"Of course I do, but it's only half as much as I love you, Bill," she hangs up the phone with a softly audible kiss.

Now, tell me that you wouldn't look forward to getting your butt home as soon as humanly possible after hearing that conversation? I dare ya, no question about it. My only concern should be getting there safely without breaking my neck! Visions of the other night are dancing in my head…Damn, obviously seeing CeCe in that negligee made a lasting imprint of my mind and then the feel of her softness as we made love well into the night.

Whew…what time is it? Crap, it's only 12:15. I still got a half a day before I can even think about getting out of there. I swing through the Chick-Fil-A and pick up a fried chicken salad plate before heading back to the office. I know, fried chicken is not the best thing to eat, but you know what? I'm under a lot of stress. I need to keep up my energy, that's for sure, so okay, so I have a little fried food, so what?

We make some small talk as Higgins and I wait patiently for John to show for the one o'clock meeting, I'm curious as to where Higgins's head is after talking to Sarah and hearing her thoughts. However, I don't ask at this point because I really don't want to cloud this investigation at all. I don't know if Milken is connected to Alice's murder at all, but everyone knows that he and I aren't the best of friends, and most would say we don't like each other at all. Besides, the HR director should be an impartial player in any investigation that involves an employee of the company, and this investigation is quite different from any other I been involved with.

"So, do you think he will show up?" Higgins asks.

"Yes, I hope so. He knows the deal, if he doesn't," I reply almost hoping he will be a no-show. Right then, the door opens and in walks Milken.

"John, this is Officer Higgins of the Metro Police. Investigator Higgins, John Milken, our warehouse director," I say to make the introductions. They shake hands, and John takes a seat across from both of us.

"Mr. Milken, thank you for coming. Just so you know, I'm the lead investigator on this case, and I'm talking to everyone who worked with Alice Randle in order to see if I can get any information that might lead us to who may have committed this crime. You are under no obligation to talk to me, however, I would appreciate it if you could answer some questions about this in hopes we can get to the bottom of this. Do I have your permission to continue sir?" Higgins states in his official capacity.

There's an awkward pause from John as if he is processing what Higgins has said. Higgins asks again, "Mr. Milken, may we proceed with the conversation?"

"Umm, am I being investigated or something? Do I need to have an attorney?" John finally mumbles.

"No, sir, Mr. Milken. You are under no obligation to speak with me at this time, but I'm really just here to get some background information on Alice Randle and any other pertinent information that could be helpful in this case. You are not being investigated nor are you under any suspicion of anything at this point," Higgins states. "But I will reserve the right to question you at a later time, if it warrants."

"Well, uh…I don't know what I could possibly tell you about what happened to Alice. I hardly knew her very well," John remarks nervously.

"Okay, thank you, sir," Higgins continues. "Sir, how long HAVE you known the deceased, Alice Randle?"

"Uh, Bill would know when she actually started here with the company; it's probably been seven or eight years, I guess," John responds.

"Okay, sir, I can get the exact date from Mr. McCallister later, but I'm just interested in when you became aware of her presence here with your company?" Higgins presses.

"Uh, well, I didn't hire her, if that's what you're asking," John says nervously.

"No sir, I'm not interested in her hiring at all at this time. I'm just curious as to when you met and was aware of Alice Randle?" Higgins restates.

"I, uh…probably saw her around after she was hired, but I don't recall exactly when I actually met her. It was most likely at an employee meeting one of my supervisors scheduled. I didn't know most of the employees until they had completed their ninety-day probationary period. Some of them came and went pretty quick, so I usually waited until they had been onboard awhile before meeting them formally," John spoke quickly, almost running his sentences together. Clearly, he was very nervous.

"Okay, sir, thank you," Higgins continues. "Um, when did you hear about the incident with Alice on the evening of the fifteenth?"

"Uh, I got a call from one of the other supervisors and the night security guard. I was awakened about 3:15 in the morning, they told me that Alice had been shot in our company parking lot. I was completely shocked and then told them I would be there just as soon as I could. I only live about twenty minutes away. I called my supervisor on my way in to see what was going on at that time, and he said the ambulance had just arrived and they were beginning to work on Alice. I kept him on the phone until I got to the parking lot just as the ambulance was leaving. I saw several employees standing outside, some were huddled up hugging each other and crying. It was not a pretty scene," John states.

"So, is there anything else you can share with me that might be helpful?" Higgins inquires.

"Uh, not that I know of," John answers. "Everyone was kind of in shock, I went to my office in the warehouse and just sat there for a bit trying to make sense of who could, who would do something like this."

"So, let me ask you, sir." Higgins leans back in his chair and pauses for a brief second. "Do you have any idea who you think might have done this to your employee, your direct report?"

"Uh, well, I know there was a threatening letter that Alice received, and she had been discussing this with the HR department. I guess Mr. McCallister can fill you in on the details, I never saw the letter. I just heard about it," John offers up.

Bingo, this opens the door for Higgins to delve deeper into the situation with the letter since John is specifically mentioned. Higgins is good. Now I see how he was able to solve all those cases.

"Yes, I have already been apprised of the letter and its contents, Mr. Milken. Can you tell me why someone would go to the trouble of accusing Alice of having slept with you in order to get the job she had been promoted to and warning her that unless she resigned her job, this would be known to company?" Higgins is on the hunt now.

"Uh, I have no idea about any of that. I, um, think there were some others in the company that didn't think she should've been promoted to the job. I, I guess they wanted to discredit her in some way," John stammers.

"But Mr. Milken, your relationship with Ms. Randle was specifically mentioned as the reason she was promoted. Why would anyone believe that to be true? Were you and her in a relationship at any time in the past or present?" Higgins is trying to establish a relationship between John and the deceased, Alice Randle.

All of a sudden, John became quiet and did not answer. He just sat looking down at his lap. Investigator Higgins asks John if he needed some time to answer his question. John then snapped back, "I don't really think I want to continue this conversation any further without a lawyer present."

"Okay, Mr. Milken," Higgins says. "That is certainly your right. However, I will reserve the right to question you further about this matter in the future."

"Uh, hold on, what do you mean? So, I guess I am under investigation. This was just a set-up to get me to admit to something I have not done," John raises his voice.

"Exactly what is it you think you have been set up to admit to, sir?" Higgins inquires.

"Having an affair with Alice Randle! I did not have anything to do with that woman. I never touched her!" John proclaims, almost screaming.

At that very instant, I can't help but be reminded of the Bill Clinton denial on primetime television that he didn't have anything to do with "that woman," Monica Lewinsky. I could almost see that crooked finger-waving liar sitting right across the table from me right now.

"Uh, Mr. Milken please," Higgins responds. "I was just referring to the letter Ms. Randle found on her doorstep the day before she was gunned down in the company parking lot. No one has accused you of anything, but you are specially referenced in a letter about how she got a promotion, and you, sir, were Ms. Randle's immediate supervisor. I'm just trying to understand the connection between you and the deceased—if it was beyond the scope of a working relationship—to determine if we need to continue this conversation downtown at police headquarters where it can be recorded. Obviously, sir, you have the right to have an attorney present, if you so desire," Investigator Higgins explains. Higgins is direct and firm, more than even I expected.

With that, John gets up from his chair and says, "Mr. Higgins, you do what you think you need to do." He then shoots a menacing look at me, turns on his heels, and opens the conference room door, disappearing down the hall.

I glance over at Higgins and say, "Well, that was interesting!"

Higgins looks up at me and says, "Obviously, there's something more here that we don't know right now, in my opinion. I did not even get to the questioning about the apparent argument she and he had earlier in the evening before her death. I will have him come down to our interrogation room, with or without an attorney. I need to get him on the record regarding his relationship with Ms. Randle and then we'll see which direction this investigation goes from here."

It sure seems like John is being evasive so even I can understand Higgins wanting to pursue this further. But I can't help but wonder what connection this has with the threatening note left on Alice's doorstep? Hmm…just seems like there is something else missing. Little did I know at that moment, it will become even more complicated and soon.

For the rest of the day, I finish reading, deleting, and responding to new emails that have appeared on my desk top. On my calendar, I notice that I have a supervisory training meeting scheduled for tomorrow that has been postponed twice already, and I have not even started to prepare for. Just great, guess I will be spending some extra time today in preparation for this—no early day for me!

After about an hour of pulling together some Excel spreadsheets and completing my PowerPoint presentation for tomorrow's training session with a dozen supervisors from different departments representing marketing, IT, accounting, and the warehouse, I let out a sigh! Finally, I can wrap things up and get on the road to my sanctuary, away from the madness here. I glance at my watch, and I notice it's 6:30. As I close down my desktop, grab my briefcase, thinking I will call CeCe from the road, my desk phone rings. Outside call, who could this be? Should I even answer? Okay, under the circumstances I don't have a choice.

"Hello," I say reluctantly.

"Mr. McCallister, this is Investigator Higgins. I just wanted you to know that we have picked up John Milken, and he is on his way here to the station for questioning. He's been read his rights, and depending on what we learn, we may be getting closer to solving this case. I just wanted you to know as I'm sure you will be asked to bring your boss and other leaders at your company in the loop."

"Wait, what?" I say in complete surprise. "What's happened? What's transpired since the conversation with John this afternoon?"

Higgins hesitates but then says, "I can't go into detail with you at this time, Mr. McCallister, but let's just say we have some damning evidence that puts Mr. Milken at the scene of Ms. Randle's murder at or near the time frame of the shooting."

"Wow, okay…thank you for letting me know," I respond in disbelief. "I guess we'll talk more tomorrow. Is there anything I need to do in the meantime, detective?"

"No, not at this time, sir. I will be in touch. Have a good evening," he says as he hangs up the phone.

Okay, I guess Sarah was right on target with her thinking about Milken. Sounds like there was something more to the relationship with Alice. Jesus, my head is spinning now as I make my way to my car and start the long drive home. I dial up CeCe and tell her the news. She is not surprised as she never really cared for John, nor his wife Maria. Women just have that sixth sense about acquaintances that men don't, especially other women. I always thought John is a royal jerk and rough around the edges, to say the least. He rarely showed much compassion for any of his employees, but I never would have ever thought he was capable of killing one of them. But then again, he is an ex-Marine. Killing was his life at one time. That cannot be denied.

Once I get home, I head straight for the liquor cabinet. If there's any day that calls for a double shot, today is that day! CeCe and I have a quiet dinner, almost as if she senses that I have serious things on my mind. And of course, I do…like what and how do we convey what's happened so far to the warehouse team members? What needs to be the prepared response to the press, which I'm certain we will be facing first thing in the morning? Who is going to be in charge of the warehouse going forward, knowing that we have these extra orders for the next few months? Carl will want to know what the game plan is—oh my God! I need to call Carl right away! I totally forgot to let him know about John. So I quickly dial up Carl.

"Hello, Bill," Carl answers after several rings. "What's up? You can't be calling me at this hour with any good news."

I glance at my watch, 10:30 p.m. "Oh, sorry, Carl," I say apologetically. "I didn't realize what time it is. I'm sorry to be calling so late, time got away, but I don't know if you're aware yet but the police have arrested John Milken and he's at the police station as we speak."

"What? What the hell?" Carl is obviously as shocked as I was after hearing the news. "So, what is he being charged with, Bill? Do you know?" Carl asks.

"I don't have that information right now, Carl. He was brought in for questioning this evening, something about evidence that puts him at or near the scene of Alice's murder around that same time," I explain.

"Jesus Christ! This is all we need right now," Carl proclaims. "And this is not what we need at this time with the extra orders we need to handle in the warehouse, Bill. We need to meet first thing in the morning, my office. In the meantime, I'll inform Sam and Sheila. You see if you can get more information on John by the morning. Let's see if we can find out the details so we can craft a plan of action."

"Yes, sir. No problem," I respond, and with that, we hang up.

For the rest of the night, I know I won't get much sleep anyway so while CeCe heads to bed, I go into the office. I start making notes on plans for tomorrow. And I thought this was a tough day! Jeez, this week just keeps getting worse and worse. Well, one thing is for sure, the week has gotten progressively worse, but it is about to get even more challenging; I just have no idea how much!

Once again, I do not have much sleep the night before, but I know things needed to be done and I couldn't wait to get into the office. So I quietly but hurriedly shower, get dressed, and swallow down a few gulps of coffee thinking I'll get another cup at the office, and since I will be there early, I can make it fresh myself...oh boy, what a big difference from the usual! Yeah, right! I kiss CeCe on the forward softly trying not to wake her and turn toward the door to leave for the office when I hear a faint voice. "Bill, please be careful...love you!" CeCe mumbles, half asleep. At that moment, I fight a very strong urge to turn around, strip off my work clothes, and climb back into the bed just spend the next two hours in a cuddled embrace with that awesome woman. But I know I have some important things to do that I cannot ignore, so I reluctantly head to the door and out into the dark of night to make the long drive into work. I must have made the trip to the office in record time as it seemed like the clock on my dash did not move much, and I was pulling into the parking lot. It helped that there weren't many cars on the road at 5:00 a.m., and for sure, I was exceeding the posted speed limit. I have a call into Higgins, but he hasn't returned my call when I walked into the office. I got to my desk without making contact with anyone so far, but it was only 5:30 in the morning, hours before anyone would be showing up for work yet. I am exhausted. I can hardly keep my eyes open, but I know I need to have some suggestions and the start of an action plan for Carl when we meet in a little while. Hopefully, Higgins would be calling with an update on what was going to happen with John Milken. Still hard to believe we've had a killer right here in our midst all this time. It is still shocking to think in those terms.

As I sit staring at my desk top, trying to think what, no, how was I going to start this document. Then I start to feel very drowsy, and the next thing I know, I am weaving. I need to put my head down on the desk for a second. Yes, if I can rest for just a minute. It seemed like I am only out asleep for maybe a minute when I begin to hear conversation coming from the outer office. I glance over at my wall clock. 7:30? What? It can't be. It seemed like it was just a minute or two. Oh, great! I fall asleep and I don't have anything for the meeting that will start when Carl gets in, probably around eight-ish. Okay, let me get focused so I can put something together. Announcement to team members, press, and deciding who will be in charge in the warehouse going forward. I couldn't help but think one of those knuckleheads who openly complained about Alice getting the assistant GM job will now have the honor of running the whole warehouse. How ironic! Okay, pressure's on, morons. Let's see what they can do now… Be careful what you ask for!

Wait a minute, the letter…the letter! John wouldn't write that letter to Alice if the two of them were linked romantically. That would call more attention to the relationship than would be necessary, why would he do that? So someone else had to be the author… but who? Who benefits most from both John and Alice being out of the way? Hmmm…I'm wondering now, is there another person involved in this altogether?

Just then, the phone rings and I answer since the caller is from the outside. Maybe it's Higgins with an update on John. "Hello, Bill McCallister," I answer, clearing my throat.

"Yes, hello, Mr. McCallister. This is Lieutenant Markle from the Metro Police. I'm calling you on behalf of Detective Higgins. He asked me to get back with you."

"Yes, I had a call into Detective Higgins," I explain. "I just wanted to get an update on the case. I understand John Milken was brought down to the station for questioning. Can you tell me if he's been charged with anything at this time? I have a meeting with our company leadership in a few minutes, and I wanted to give them an update."

"Well, sir, Mr. Milken is being questioned at the present time. He was arrested late yesterday, but he has not been charged with anything as of the moment. By law, we have the right to hold him up to forty-eight hours before either a charge has to be made or we will be required to release him," Markle explains.

"Oh, I see. So he has not been charged at this time?" I ask.

"No, sir. Not at the moment. But he is being questioned with his attorney present. I'm sure Detective Higgins will get back with you at his earliest opportunity," Markle explains.

"Okay, thank you for the update, lieutenant," I say and hang up the phone. So nothing definitely on John at this time. Knowing John's demeanor, I'm sure he's hanging tough with his attorney under stressful interrogation. Wish I could be a fly on the wall… Higgins gives me the impression he can be a bull in a china shop when necessary. Poor John Milken, I wouldn't want to be him right now, no, sir!

Just then, Rosie taps on my door lightly, I motion her in with my left hand as I'm covering a yawn with the other.

"Good morning, Mr. McCallister. I hope you're having a good day. I noticed you were in early today. We have several newspeople in the main lobby asking to talk with someone in authority. They would like to speak with Mr. Johnson, but Jayne has instructed me that Mr. Johnson is not meeting with anyone right now and he is currently unavailable," she says, more serious than I ever recall.

"Thank you, Rosie, but we are not talking to the press right now. I have a meeting with Mr. Johnson at eight this morning, and we'll decide something from there," I explain.

"Okay, Mr. McCallister, I understand," Rosie responds. "But I also had a call from Maria Milken this morning, and she would like to have a few words with you, at your earliest convenience."

"Uh…Maria Milken?" I ask.

"Yes sir, she said it was vitally important that she speak with you right away," Rosie said.

"Uh, okay, I guess," I slowly say. "But I won't be able to see her until later this afternoon, no earlier than 2:00 p.m. please," I tell her.

"All right, sir. I will set her up for a time after 2:00 this afternoon and put it on your calendar," Rosie turns and walks away.

Before I can even get focused, Sarah sticks her head in and says, "Good morning, got a sec?"

"Actually no, Sarah, I'm sorry. I have to get some things together for Carl, and I don't have much time," I say without even looking up.

"No problem, boss. We can chat when you have a minute. I just need to fill you in on a conversation I had with my brother about that drug gang they busted in the warehouse last year. Your name came up in their investigations, and he wanted me to alert you," she says quickly and starts to walk away.

"Huh? Wait, what? Sarah, come back? What are you saying? My name? What are you talking about?" I sound like a desperate quiz show contestant trying to clarify clues to the million-dollar question.

"Okay, well Tommy, my brother, called me last night and said he needed to bring us up to speed on their investigation on the drug ring that was operating in our warehouse last year," she starts.

"Yes, yes, okay, but what about my name? Why is my name coming up in this investigation?" I ask with obvious anxiousness.

"Okay, he said that they had uncovered email correspondence from one of the drug dealers with unknown participants on a laptop that had confiscated where your name was being discussed as the person who involved Law Enforcement which busted their activities here at ODI. I just thought you would want to know this right away," Sarah says.

"What does that mean?" I ask. "Am I some sort of a target for this group? Was there anything else that I need to be worried about?"

"Uh, I'm not sure, Mr. McCallister, but maybe we should be asking my brother about that. He does want to talk with us and bring us up to date on the matter when it's convenient for us," Sarah says with a shrug of her shoulders.

Hmmm, now I'm not sure how to take what she has just told me. Is my life in danger with this group of drug dealers? "Uh, Sarah, right now, I have to get some things together for Carl, but I really want to find out what your brother is referring to regarding my name on email correspondence they have uncovered. Can we set something up this afternoon, uh…how about after 3:00 p.m.? I'm meeting with

John Milken's wife this afternoon at two, so if he can take a call at that time or later, that will be good for me," I say with a worried tone.

"I will try and arrange the call for three with Tommy, sir, but please don't give it another thought. I'm sure it's nothing to worry about," Sarah replies.

But it was clear she was trying to console me, probably thinking she alarmed me for no reason with her previous statement. Great, now I may have some drug dealers and who knows a drug cartel out there gunning for my head all because we busted up their sweetheart drug ring here at work. Damn, I never thought HR work would ever become hazardous to your health or a threat on your life. Sure, human emotion can lead people to do some crazy things, even commit bodily harm and empty threats of violence; but in the workplace, actual violence is generally not that common. At least, I never thought about it that way, especially when it was about myself. I literally throw some information down on a document and printed copies for my meeting with Carl, Sam, Sheila, and whoever else he is going to have join us. I assume there might be others so I have ten copies made, just in case. I enter the outer offices to the CEO and I could already hear Sam's loud voice before I even said anything to Jayne.

"Hi, Jayne. Carl is expecting me," I say as I pass her desk.

"Yes, sir. Please go right in," Jayne responds.

I walk into the meeting in Carl's office, and there is Sam, Sheila, and someone else I didn't recognize from the back right away, all facing Carl's desk in a semi-circle. As I come around to the empty chair, I then recognize our CFO, David Smith, as the third person in attendance.

"Good morning, Bill," they all say, almost in unison.

"Good morning," I respond.

Carl looks up at me and says, "Sam was explaining how he thinks we should decide who will be the person in charge of the warehouse for the time being. As we all know, the new orders will hit next week, and we have to have our ducks in a row. This could be the beginning of something really big for ODI, as the client has signaled that if we can provide the product as stipulated in the contract on time, then there very well could be another large order coming our way." Carl is explaining in a very upbeat manner.

"So, Bill," Carl asks, "what constraints do we need to clear in order to put someone in charge of the warehouse on a temporary basis until this thing with John gets settled?"

Obviously, with a surprised look on my face, I respond, "Actually, Carl there aren't any legal issues that would prevent us from assigning whomever we want into a temporary leadership role in the warehouse, given the circumstances. However, there might a perception issue we should consider."

"How so?" Sam bellows. "Who would care?" he continues, looking directly at Carl.

"Yes, please explain, Bill," Carl echoes.

"Well, given the sensitivity of what has happened, and the fact that the current warehouse director is being investigated for murder, I think it is important that we choose a person who can keep the peace out there and who will be seen as a credible leader since this is apparently a very important client and product order that might lead to further business down the road," I say confidently, still surprised that this is what we're discussing instead of how to respond to the clamor for information from team members and the press.

"He has a good point," David, the CFO pipes up, spoken from someone with a true financial interest.

"However, I was under the impression we would be discussing how to respond to the team members and the press about what has transpired recently," I say bluntly.

"Yes, yes, we will get to that, Bill, but having the right person in charge out there in the meantime is most essential," Carl responds. "Besides, Sheila will draft language for a news release to the press and then she will work with you and your team on holding employee meetings with the warehouse group to address their fears and concerns," Carl announces as if everything has already been predetermined.

"Getting back to your concerns, Bill, how should we go about making the determination as to who we assign into the temporary leadership role?" he continues.

As I'm sitting there, mulling through in my mind how important the next few weeks are to ODI and the quality of supervision with the potential candidates—or should I say, lack of qualified potential candidates—it dawns on me that maybe we would benefit with supreme expertise in the warehouse over the next few weeks in order to ensure we meet the order deadline, so without hesitation, I blurt out, "How about Sam overseeing the warehouse operations during this crucial time as it is so vitally important that we satisfy this client's order and procuring a possible windfall for future orders from them? This would also help to settle down the personnel out there with a member of the executive management team running the operation. Besides, it's just for the duration of this order, and in the meantime, it will give us time to decide on who should be considered as a potential replacement for John Milken, if he is not able to return to his job."

"Whoa, there. Hold on, chief. I'm not qualified to run the warehouse. It's not my expertise," objects Sam.

"Hang on a minute, Sam," Carl interjects. "Maybe that is our best option for the time being. That way, we accomplish what Bill is saying and gives us time to see how this thing with Milken is going to playout. Besides, we cannot drop the ball on this order, no way whatsoever. It's too important to ODI's future," Carl announces as if it is already a done deal.

I glance over at Sam, and he is glaring at me out of the side of his face.

"I agree with that decision, Carl," David speaks up. Sheila nods her head up and down as she makes notes.

"Excellent. That settles it," Carl says. "Let's put together an announcement on Sam and then work on the press release."

"Way ahead of you, sir," Sheila speaks up. Meanwhile, I feel Sam's stern gaze on the left side of my face as he gets up and turns to walk out the door. Sheila glances over at me with a look of approval, taps me on the shoulder, and then turns and exits Carl's office.

David gets up, leans over my way, and says, "Great suggestion, Bill."

I start to rise from my chair, and Carl says to me, "Bill, stay seated please. Don't go anywhere just yet," as he gets up to close his door and returns to his chair. "Listen, I really appreciate your insight and quick thinking on this matter, Bill. That was an excellent suggestion. It accomplishes a lot of concerns and buys us time to decide our next move, which is exactly what we need right now."

"Thank you, sir, but I'm not so sure Sam is happy about the decision. I was just throwing it out there for discussion," I respond.

"Oh, don't worry," Carl starts off, "he will be fine. It makes the most sense. We do not have anyone else out there, thanks to Milken, who I can trust to effectively run that warehouse especially during this upcoming critical time. I just wanted you to know how much I appreciate and value your expertise. Thank you, Bill."

I leave Carl's office wondering what just happened, as what I suggested just seemed logical to me. Having one of those yahoos Milken put into supervision over the years into the primary warehouse leadership role, even on a temporary basis, could be and would be dangerous, in my opinion. I know Sam would not be in favor of being chosen to run the warehouse, but it is only real option we have, under the circumstances. I will have to mend that fence in the coming weeks. Oh, what the hell...I'm out of here in a couple of years anyway. Does it really matter? Like Carl said, Sam will be fine...and if not, so be it.

The meeting with Maria Milken is set for 2:00 p.m. today but I really have no idea what to expect or why this woman requested an audience with me. As a personal rule, I normally don't meet with spouses without the team member being present. However, due to the circumstances surrounding John and his alleged involvement with Alice's death, I am somewhat curious as to why the urgent request, as she mentioned to Rosie.

It does cross my mind that she may be inquiring about possibly of withdrawing money from John's 401(k) account to help with the legal costs. Obviously, on several previous occasions, I have met with employees asking for information and the procedure for taking money out of their retirement accounts for emergency purposes. I wasn't sure if hiring an attorney met the qualifications for obtaining a hardship withdrawal from a 401(k) given the restrictive rules of the IRS. I am sure that John could apply for a loan from his 401(k), as many team members have done in the past, paying back the loan through regular payroll deduction. I will need to research the program in advance of my meeting with John's wife. Not knowing her very well outside of a few company functions, I got the distinct impression she was a demanding woman which always made the whole relationship with John seem odd to me. Since he isn't very personable himself, I just couldn't see the two of them having anything near the special relationship CeCe and I enjoyed. I recall CeCe making a similar comment about the two of them following a company event in the past. Even though I had some reservation about the meeting with Maria Milken, little did I know at that moment what I was going to experience, not in the least. My world was about to get impacted in a very big way, one I did not see coming at all.

The front desk receptionist buzzes me that Maria is here for her 2:00 appointment. Glancing at my watch, I noticed it was only 1:45.

"Well, she's very early," I told Sue, our receptionist. "Please have her take a seat, and I will be with her as soon as I can."

As I hang up the phone, I can't help but think that her being this early for our appointment is just typical behavior for a type A personality, always anxious about everything. I continue reading about the IRS rules for hardship withdrawals and loans from 401(k) accounts, making sure I could give her accurate advice to share with John. About ten minutes later, Rosie appears at my door and says that Sue, at the front desk, buzzed her to ask if Maria Milken can come wait in our conference room until I am ready to meet with her. She told Rosie that Maria is nervously pacing back and forth the lobby, obviously very distracting to other guests.

I look up at Rosie and say in a very frustrated tone, "What is with this woman? We have a two o'clock appointment, and it's only 1:56"—looking at my watch—"Can she wait another few minutes and I will be with her as soon as I get finished here? Look, Rosie, I'm sorry, I just need to finish looking up some information for her before we meet."

"Oh, no problem, Mr. McCallister. I understand. No apology necessary. Perhaps she can wait in our conference room, it will be less distracting to the other guests?" Rosie suggests.

"Sure, sure, that's fine Rosie, but please let her know that I really need to finish what I'm doing first before we can meet and remind her that our appointment is not until 2:00 p.m.," I say, shaking my head.

"Of course, I'll go get her and escort her into the conference room and let her know you will be with just as soon as you can, sir," Rosie beams in her usual pleasant way.

Thank God I was almost finished with my research, anyway, so I could go ahead and get this meeting over. I have so many other things to do today before I can even think about leaving and going home to the sanctuary of my personal world.

Before having Rosie get Maria and bring her to my office, I fire off a quick email to Sheila explaining that it would be best if we got together first thing in the morning about drafting a notice to warehouse team members and developing a meeting schedule. I do not know how long I will be tied up with Maria, and I have some other things I need to get done before the day was over. I have not even had a chance to consult with Sarah about plans for the warehouse or call our labor attorney to bring him up to speed on the most recent events. Sheila will just have to wait. Right now, I need to meet with this impatient woman, which I am now regretting, and hoping that the uncomfortable feeling in the pit of my stomach is just the fried chicken I had for lunch.

I buzz Rosie to let her know to bring Maria back to my office. As I stand up and start to come around my desk to greet Maria, my phone rings and I think it best to answer since I expecting a call from Investigator Higgins. He had called earlier that morning about coming by to see me because he had something important that he needed to share with me in person. Seems like this was one of those days where everyone is going to be secretive and coy about meeting with me.

Why can't people just be open and honest about their motives? I wonder. "Hello," I answer.

"Mr. McCallister, this is Officer Higgins. I'm about ten minutes away from your office, is it possible we can meet right away? I really need to see you, it is urgent," he says with little emotion. But that was his style, very matter-of-fact and to the point, which is why I have grown to like him during this whole ordeal.

I start to answer just as Maria is being escorted into my office, and as I look at her coming through the door, I cannot even find the words to respond to Officer Higgins. I can hardly believe what I was seeing!

Maria is very tightly wrapped in a silky white low-cut blouse and a red-lined skintight mini-skirt that when I say is short, I mean dictionary definition short! She has on very high heel shoes with thin laced black stockings that clearly accentuated her long legs. Her long jet-black hair is draped flowingly around her shoulders, and with her make-up, she appeared like she had just stepped out of the salon. It seemed she was better dressed to hit the club scene. Now, I have to say, this woman is well into her forties, but she can easily pass for someone much younger.

"Mr. McCallister, you there?" I hear Officer Higgins in my ear.

"Uh, yes, I'm here. Sorry, someone just came into my office. Whenever you get here, just have the receptionist notify Rosie," I say, barely hearing my own words.

"Great, see you soon, sir," I hear the phone clicks, but with it still next to my ear, I slowly mouth a response that didn't seem to make any sense even to me; I don't even know what I said. Hanging up the phone and collecting myself, I turn to Maria.

"Please have a seat, Maria. Good to see you again. I'm so sorry to hear about John," I say as I sit down.

"Thank you, Mr. McCallister. I really appreciate you making time to meet with me today," she said in a low tone.

"Of course, I know things have not been great with John's situation. It hasn't been good for anyone. How can I help you today?" I ask, expecting her to inquire about the 401(k) options.

"Well, you know the circumstances Mr. McCallister," she says very slowly and leaning over toward me from her chair, giving me full view of her ample cleavage.

"It's not good. Definitely not a good time for anyone right now. You know John is innocent, he could never do what the police are saying, not in a million years," she says in one breath.

"Uh, well, I don't think he has been charged with anything, officially, right? I believe he's just being held for questioning, for like forty-eight hours. I assume he will be getting an attorney, correct?" I say with a puzzled look.

"No, nothing definite right now and I guess they have the right by law to keep him for forty-eight hours before they have to either charge him or let him go," she mused. "But I'm not here to debate that. I just needed to talk with someone, and with you being the HR Director for the company, I'm hoping you can influence the police on John's behalf? I mean, John has been with ODI for many years, most of his adult life, and he's never had an issue or problem with anyone here. If you were to write a reference or give the police some kind of letter of support for John, wouldn't that help him?" she says inquisitively.

"Uh, Maria, I'm not sure that's appropriate right now. First of all, as we've agreed, John has not been charged with anything, and this is an official police investigation. All ODI can do at this point is respond to their questions, provide the required information as requested. It would be highly out of order for the company to make any judgements at this time. Let's just see where all this goes. Hopefully, John will satisfy the police, and he will be released soon to come back home. If you're worried about John keeping his job or any impact on his future here at ODI, please let me assure you that we are not in a position to make a determination at this point. It would be premature for us to take any action right now," I say in my best official tone.

"But, but," she stammered, "it would be helpful to John if his company supported him while he is going through this, right? After all, like you said, he has not been charged with a crime at this point. They're just telling me that he's a person of interest, whatever that means, and they have the right to hold him for questioning." She is almost crying now and looking down.

I offer her a tissue from the box I keep on my desk for just such occasions. "Okay, look, Maria. ODI just cannot get involved in supporting anyone at this time, as it wouldn't make a difference anyway. Let's just allow the police investigation play itself out, but in the meantime, nothing will change as far as John's employment with ODI," I say with empathy.

Maria looks up wiping her eyes with the tissue and smiles, showing her obviously recently polished white teeth.

"Well, what if we could work something out?" she says seductively, sticking out her chest. "Is there anything I can do for you that will change your mind? Anything?"

All of a sudden, it dawns on me what is really going on here and why the urgency to see me and the provocative dressing for the occasion. This woman is trying to seduce me into doing a favor which she believes will benefit her husband. Seriously? What is wrong with her? I'm totally floored by the suggestion that she is willing to do whatever it takes for me to write a letter on John's behalf. All along, I thought maybe she was here to see about getting some of John's retirement money for an attorney, and she's here to get me, or ODI, to come out in support of her husband when the police obviously believe he had something to do with Alice Randal's murder. Unbelievable!

"Uh, Maria, umm…I'm flattered by your suggestion. No, wait…I'm not flattered, I'm shocked, and honestly, I'm totally disappointed right now," I say tersely. "You actually came in here to meet with me expecting to convince me to do something you want and then you'll do whatever and anything I want in return? Seriously? I'm sorry, but I'm going to end this conversation now."

I barely got the words out when she stands up and leans over my desk. She then starts to scream in a very loud voice. "You asshole, you want me to suck you off in your office or else you will have the police to press charges against my husband?" she screams.

Right then and there, I realized the cardinal sin I made by not asking someone else sit in with me on this conversation with this woman. I stand up and head for the door, she steps in front of me and screams again, "No sir, I will not do sexual favors for you, no matter if you fire my husband, you pig! I'm not that kind of woman!" she yells.

About this time, Sarah opens my door, "What is going on? What happened?" She steps in between me and Maria, who is now inches from my face. Maria begins to yell that I threatened to get rid of John and make up lies if she didn't let me have sex with her.

At that moment, several of my staff appear at my door, looking shocked and perplexed after hearing Maria's screaming and yelling. Sarah looks at me in shock and says, "Mr. McCallister, what happened?"

By this time, Maria has sat back down and is holding her head in her hands sobbing uncontrollably. I look at Sarah and say, "Sarah, this woman came in here today to explicitly to offer sex to me in exchange for a letter to the police in support for John, and when I refused, she started screaming that I was asking her for sex."

Maria, stops her crying to look up at Sarah and says, "That's not true. Your boss asked me to sleep with him or else he would tell the police a bunch of lies about John if I did not do what he wanted. He has never liked John. Ask anyone. Everybody knows how much you hate him; you've made it very clear." She says this very clear and very composed, obviously well-aware that most of my staff had squeezed into my office listening to her every word with quiet anticipation.

Right then, I notice Officer Higgins is standing in the background as he had responded to Maria's screaming and ranting. I lean over to Sarah and whisper, "Why don't you take Maria to your office so we can get things settled down? Thank you."

"Yes, sir, good idea. Ms. Milken please come with me." Sarah is quick to respond, reaching for Maria's elbow, escorting her out of my office. While most of those who came to see what had happened files out of my office, Rosie stays behind. Officer Higgins steps in as Rosie is saying she just knew I would never do the things Maria had said.

"Well, Mr. McCallister, it certainly looks like you're going to have your hands full now. I don't see her just going away after that outburst... I'd say she has other intentions. I'm sure you haven't heard the end of this," he says with a slight smirk on his face.

"Oh, so you heard what she said, right?" I ask.

"Of course, so did everyone else in this side of the building, I'm afraid," he responds.

Wow, I certainly wasn't expecting anything like this. How embarrassing! In front of my staff, the HR director, their boss, being accused of soliciting sexual favors? Oh brother, what else can happen today? Of all the things to happen, sexual impropriety should never be what any HR person is accused of. Hell, HR professionals are supposed to be the shining star model for all employees in that regard. We hold the organization responsible for maintaining a safe and sexual harassment-free environment. Obviously I violated a cardinal rule of HR procedure by not having another person in the room when conferring with a member of the opposite sex, especially under the present circumstances. In my defense, hmm...hell, I have no defense. I even thought about it before she came in. It was just pure stupidity. You would think I'd know better after all these years. Ah, another sign, the end cannot be far away.

"So tell me, Officer Higgins, what was it you just had to see me for in person today?" I say sarcastically.

"Well," he says, as he closes the door. "You know we are questioning your warehouse manager in the case of the murdered employee, and just so you know, we now have video footage of his vehicle traveling along I-60 through a toll gate heading in the direction of your building during the early morning hours of January 9, the same date and approximately around the same time Alice Randle was gunned down. Based on that information, he's going to be charged with the murder of Ms. Randle as the district attorney believes with this video confirmation, coupled with eyewitness accounts of an argument on the premises between Mr. Milken and the deceased earlier that evening, elevates his level of involvement in the case. However, I really need to ask Ms. Milken a few questions, if you don't mind. I see she is still in your associate's office. I'll be right back," he says as he turns to exit my office.

"Officer Higgins?" I shout.

"Yes?" he turns and replies.

"Whatever you do, keep Sarah in there with you!" I advise.

"Don't worry. No way I'm talking to that woman without a witness," he remarks with another smirk on his face.

As Higgins left my office, I couldn't help but wonder what could possibly be next in store for me today. What else could happen? I feel elated that I had pleased my boss by suggesting a plan that would both benefit the company and our team members and was told that my contributions were much appreciated, and then ironically, later that same day, I was accused of sexual harassment in front of my staff by obviously an unhinged woman with a distinct motive. These are the days that give you such a dichotomy of strange feelings deep within that can confuse your soul. I have experienced the full spectrum of emotion, all in one day! Or so, I thought.

I thought it best to go tell my boss, Carl, what had just transpired in my office with John Milken's wife, not that I had any guilt or remorse for anything I did, but just in case he heard about the event from someone else. Carl would expect me to tell him myself, I'm sure of that. As I approach his office, I turn the last corner and who do I run smack into but Sam Morris.

"Well, well, well," in a sarcastic tone, obviously coming from Carl's office making a last-ditch effort to get him to change his mind about the assignment. "Look who it is. The guy who suggested I take the lead in the warehouse instead of someone else who actually lives out there."

"Look, Sam, all I did was suggest an option. I didn't make the call. Besides, who knows more about the warehouse than you? You have intimate knowledge of how things work out there, more than anyone else I know. You have to admit that the supervisors aren't capable of running that place especially with this important order to fill," I respond, defending myself.

"Sure, you're not the one who will have to live out there for the next few weeks, day and night, just to be sure those clowns don't fuck things up. Thanks a lot!" he angrily growls as he walks away.

"I rest my case," I snap back and disappear into the executive outer offices. Seems like everybody wants to complain about their work, but nobody wants to take any personal responsibility. This guy ultimately oversees the entire warehouse function, you'd think he'd want it to be sure things run smoothly over the next few weeks, since our boss has made it crystal clear it is his and ODI's main priority.

As I enter the CEO's office for a second time today—believe me, not because I really wanted to—I see him deep into his desktop reviewing performance reports no doubt. Hell, he could be looking at pornography for all I care. I am getting ready to inform him that his top HR person for the company was just accused of soliciting sex from the wife of his warehouse director, who is being formally charged with the murder of his assistant warehouse director for who knows the reason why! Hey seriously, you just can't make this stuff up!

After informing Carl of the events in my office—and hearing him repeat for the third time that he couldn't believe that I did not have another person arrange to sit in the meeting with me—I tuck my tail between my legs and make my way back to my office fully knowing that if John's wife really wanted to make my life miserable, all she had to do was reach out to one of those ambulance-chasing labor attorneys and then it would my word against hers. Even if I was eventually exonerated, my pristine reputation would definitely take a hit. How much? That remains to be seen. As I walk past Rosie's desk, reentering the HR offices, Rosie looks up from her phone and says, "Mr. McCallister, I have Tom Robbins from the State on the phone says he has a 3:00 p.m. call with you and Sarah, but she's in with Detective Higgins, shall I take a message or have him call back?"

"Uh, no, Rosie, please let him know I need a couple of minutes. I'll pick the line up in my office. Thank you."

"Sure thing, Mr. McCallister." Then she turns back to the call to put him on a brief hold. I get back into my office and plop down in my chair, take a deep breath and pick up the phone pressing the blinking line.

"Tom, this is Bill McCallister. I apologize for the wait, but Sarah is tied up on another matter. If you are of with just talking with me, I understand there was some information you have uncovered in the drug ring investigation?" I ask inquisitively.

"Yes, sir, this is Tom Robbins. I had mentioned to Sarah last night that while wrapping up our investigation of the drug ring that was operating in your warehouse last year, we came across some email traffic on a confiscated laptop that implicates you as a potential target for your role in setting up the undercover sting that led to the arrest of those involved in that drug activity at your facility."

"Uh, target? Mr. Robbins, what exactly does that mean? Am I in some sort of danger?" I ask.

"Well, honestly, Mr. McCallister, we're not sure exactly what this means as there are no details or specifics that identify any plan of action, but I wanted you to be aware that your name was in an email. At this point, we do not have information on the recipient of the email yet, but we know it was generated by one of the gang members that was arrested at your facility last September. It does not specify any plan or plot to cause you any harm, but I thought it was something you should be aware of." He goes on to say.

"Okay, should I be concerned for my welfare at this point, or am I being too sensitive?" I inquire with obvious interest.

"Ah, Mr. McCallister, there is absolutely no imminent threat of harm at this point, but we are still working this case; and if we find any reason whatsoever to believe there is something you should know in order to protect yourself, we will be in touch. I realize that receiving a call like this can be unsettling," he states.

Right then the words, YA THINK? stream through my brain.

"However, until we get more clarity on this matter or uncover anything else that leads us to believe you may be in danger, we will inform you as soon as possible. Since my little sister works for you and your company, I just thought you would want to know what we know at this point, but I really don't have anything else concrete to share at this time. If you give me your cell phone number, I will personally keep you informed the minute anything develops that we believe you need to know. Obviously, you're a smart man, just continue to go about your life, as usual but be aware that there are dangers out there in the world and protect yourself accordingly," he advises.

"Sure thing, Mr. Robbins. I appreciate the heads-up, and please don't hesitate to contact me the second you know anything further. My cell phone is 455-507-3365. Thank you for the advice. Goodbye." I hang up the phone.

Okay, nothing specific other than to advise me that my name was found on a computer confiscated by law enforcement, but why would one of ODI's former employees and drug dealer be sending my name to an email contact as the person responsible for calling in law enforcement to break up their drug here at work? Actually, I had very little to do with establishing the sting operation, either setting it up or monitoring the activity. It was all secret, and Carl and I were only given weekly briefings. Yes, I was aware and involved from the beginning but so were several other individuals, but these idiots would not know any of that…sometimes with just being in my position, you get the blame. Comes with the territory. Okay, I'm not going to get over concerned here, besides like he said, there is no imminent threat of harm at this point. I don't want to read too much into this, but it does give me a solid reason to be more aware of my surroundings when I am out and about. I must tell CeCe about this as well…just so she can do the same. You can't always anticipate what desperate people might do under desperate situations. What a day…but I tried to warn you. Such is the life of a human resources professional. Well, maybe not the norm EVERY day, but it seems to be more often than not when you consistently deal with those who dwell at the bottom of the character spectrum. It comes with the territory, I guess.

I make my way through the office corridor to the rear door of our building in my desire to get home to the comforting confines of my personal sanctuary—home. Glancing at my watch, I notice it's already past 7:00 p.m. Where has the day gone? Fun and games almost all day long, can't wait to get home tonight. CeCe will definitely be a welcome sight to see, for sure.

Just then my cell phone rings; it's CeCe. "Hi, hon, I'm on my way right now" but I get no further, as CeCe is already speaking on the other end and quite loudly, I might add. "What is going on, Bill?" CeCe says, very demanding. "I found this note on our door saying that you were asking for sexual favors from Maria Milken?" Her voice is cracking. "What does this mean?" "Wait, what? Seriously?" I responded, trying to understand how she can possibly know what happened with Maria so soon. "CeCe, CeCe, listen to me," I pleaded, "it's not true. This is absolutely false. What exactly did this note say?", I asked. There was a long pause as I could tell she was re-reading whatever she had in her possession. "Bill, I just went out to water the plants on the front porch and found this note taped to the door", she explained. "The doorbell never rang; I did not hear anyone come to door at all. The note says that you asked Maria Milken to sleep with you and that if she didn't then you would tell lies to the police about John and the woman who worked for him, uh, Alice is her name, the one that was shot in the parking lot at your work. Bill, I know you don't care for this man but how does any of this have anything to do with you? "CeCe, there is no connection to me", I answered, "this is something being made up to throw the police off track. I don't know why but someone thinks they can pull me into this mess by making a false accusation about John's wife and me." By now I could sense that CeCe was calming down as she began to suspect that something wasn't exactly adding up from the ridiculousness of what she was reading. I sighed and said, "Ok, CeCe, come on you know me, I would never do anything like that...never!" Look, I'm on my way home and I'll fill you in on the details of what happened here today in my office. It's completely ridiculous but it will all make sense when I get there, just trust me. This is all a plan to discredit me and take the spotlight off John Milken who is being charged with Alice Randle's murder. CeCe pauses for a moment and then says, "Ok Bill, we'll talk when you get here, drive safe."

As I walk out the door and across the parking lot, I'm trying to figure out how this note got delivered to my home so fast, it's over an hour's drive from here. Wait a minute, this whole charade in my office with Maria was obviously planned well before she came to see me. She knew exactly my what my reaction would to be to her provocative advances. I'm the HR leader for the company, for Christ's sake I couldn't be any more predictable. Still though, this just doesn't make any sense to me. Why discredit me? What made Maria think that falsely claiming a sexual advance by the HR Director and how that could possibly help John? Little did I know but I was about to find out the answer to that question, a lot sooner than I expected."

I slide into the car and turn on the ignition. As I pull out of the parking lot and onto the street, I can't help but notice a vehicle parked just beyond the entrance quickly flips on its lights as I pass. The driver then guns the vehicle, a dark-colored mid-size sedan, to get right behind me even cutting off another car coming up fairly fast from behind us.

Something didn't seem right with this, I am thinking as I reach for my cell phone in my briefcase. However, in my haste, I knock the briefcase off the passenger seat and onto the floor, out of my reach. Damn it! Okay, what do I do now? We're doing about 50 mph and a sudden stop would surely cause an accident. I can't even slow down or brake with the traffic moving so briskly in my lane. Okay, don't panic. Just keep driving...maybe this is just a coincidence. Hopefully, the driver in the vehicle behind me just wants to get home too, like me. It's about four miles on the street that runs in front of our office building before reaching the interstate on-ramp. If I can make it to the interstate, I'll know for sure if the person in this vehicle is actually following me.

The vehicle is almost riding my rear bumper now. Now I know something is not right with this, so I'm not sure about getting on the interstate. Keeping this driver behind me might be the best thing. Otherwise, if it gets beside me, they could try and run me off the road. My mind is racing now! Who is this and why are they following me so closely?

Just then, I hear a loud pop and the shattering of glass and the thump of an object hitting into my dash. I'm no expert on gunshots, but it doesn't take much to realize that someone just took a shot at me. Then, there's another loud pop and the front windshield of my car spider cracks blurring my vision of the road in front of me. I can't go any further; I have to slow down and pull over. My God, I can't see anything! The headlights behind me are blinding!

I hit the brakes and swerve hard over to the right-hand shoulder—which has a bike lane, thank God. As I come to a sliding stop, the car behind me passes by and pulls over about fifty yards ahead. I hear the screeching of tires as the line of cars behind are stopping for all the confusion. Just then I see the figure of a person exit the car that was behind me before but now stopped in front of me, but I can't make out who it is from the headlights of oncoming traffic and the vehicle lights behind me. I quickly unbuckle my seat belt and throw the car door open. If someone thinks they're going to shoot at me again, it won't be while I'm strapped into a front seat with no escape. Whoever this is will have to chase me down.

I quickly turn and run past the rear of my car toward the vehicles stopped behind me. I don't stop running and look back until I have gone past about ten cars. I stop and turn only to see this thin-framed figure running toward me. I cannot make out who this could be, but I'm not hanging around to find out. I was an athletic sort of guy back in my younger years, but at sixty-three years old, I am in no shape or condition to outrun anyone younger than me, but I am not about to stand up to someone shooting a gun at me, I don't care how old they are. I'm running with all my ability now and surprised that I am moving at a pretty quick pace. Amazing how fast adrenaline can move your ass, if need be. Whoever this is will have to run me down to catch me otherwise. I'm sure not hanging around to see who it might be.

Just then a guy who has stopped about twenty cars behind mine shoves open his car door right into my path, and I hit it broadside, causing me to slam my left leg into the door and knocking me onto the road. I roll over and over until I came to rest at the wheel of another vehicle parked in the adjacent lane. Dazed and dizzy, I sit up with my back on the tire, trying to move my obviously damaged hurt leg. I cannot feel anything in the leg, but I can see my right arm is covered in blood from the road rash I sustained in the fall and roll. Obviously, several vehicles are stopped because of the confusion ahead of them.

Suddenly, a figure appears about thirty feet in front of me. I can hardly make out who it is but as the figure slowly moves toward me, I can clearly see it is Maria Milken. What the hell? She raises her arm, and I see a small gun in her right hand. Oh God, this woman is going to shoot me. Why?

Just then a loud popping noise happens, echoing off the parked cars around me, and then almost simultaneously, another one louder than the previous. I feel huge pressure in my right upper chest area like a weighted blanket is draped over my shoulder and my shirt starts to turn crimson red. I look toward where Maria is last standing, but I do not see her any more. I begin to feel extremely nauseous and then everything starts to turn black. I can't see anything. Is this it? Is this how I will die? Really? As I contemplate what has transpired in just the last week of my life, it dawns on me that maybe I've been asking myself the wrong question. Instead of when will I be "Getting to the End" perhaps I should be asking, "What the hell's next?" After all, I still have two more years of this circus fun house to go! Surely, the future can't be any more bizarre or dangerous, right? Guess we'll see as I shift my position in the bed with a painful reminder that the next few weeks will be challenging enough indeed.

Finale

I slowly wake to total darkness and then I hear what sounds like distant voices talking in low tones. As I begin to open my eyes, the bright light seems blazingly blinding, and I am forced to squint really hard, but I still can't make out anything recognizable. Then very slowly things begin to come into focus. My muddled mind wonders if I have actually passed on to the hereafter. Is this what life after death is all about? I instinctively move my head slightly to the right toward the sound of the voices. Almost immediately, I feel my right arm and shoulder tightly bound and immovable. My left leg feels like it has the weight of something heavy on top of it, holding it firmly in place.

Just then, I hear a woman's voice. "He's waking from the sedative, I'll go let the doctor know he is coming around."

And then another female comes close to my side. "Bill, Bill, are you awake? You've had quite an ordeal... We weren't sure you were going to make it...but you are going to be all right now," the familiar, soft voice spoke and I recognized it as Steph's, Dave's wife.

Am I really alive? I wonder. Things still seemed so strange. As she leaned over to me, I could see the vague outline of Steph's face.

"Steph," I mouth. "Uh...what happened to me? The last thing I can remember was being in the road and someone, a woman... Maria Milken was trying to kill me. Where am I? Is this a dream?"

Steph whispers, "Shhh...Bill, you don't need to talk right now. There's plenty of time for that later. I'm here, and the doctor is on his way. Now, just slowly sip this water for me," as she places a straw to my lips.

I sip the water hungrily through the straw, wincing as it flows down my throat. My throat feels like it is on fire.

"Yes, your throat is very dry from the surgery, Bill. You were intubated and that caused your throat to be irritated," she explains.

I cannot move, as I do not have any strength in my arms or legs. I can just barely move my head to the side. I whisper the words, "Where's CeCe?"

Steph looks at me, smiles, and says, "Now, no talking yet. You are still too weak. CeCe will be here soon. She's just down the hall. We have been right here by your side for the last three days."

Just then, I see CeCe coming into the room with tears in her eyes. She comes to me and puts her hand lightly on my forehead. I open my eyes wider and notice her face is fraught with anguish as if she hasn't slept for days.

"Oh, Bill. You're finally awake. I knew you would! The doctor said it might take a while. It's been three days, but you are finally conscious, thank God! We really worried you wouldn't wake up." Her voice is shaking, almost sobbing.

I can clearly see where I am. It is a hospital bed with what seems like all kinds of wires and the monitors attached to me and vanilla surroundings of a hospital room.

"The kids. Jimmy and Olivia? Are they here? Are they okay?" I ask.

"Bill, the kids are just fine. Worried about you like all of us. They're staying at our house and coming soon. They both got time off from their jobs to be here for you."

I notice Steph with phone in hand, sending a text no doubt. "I just sent your kids and Dave a note, letting them know you're awake," Steph announces. "They're on the way."

I see a table full of flowers, balloons, and cards to the left by the window. CeCe says everyone—Charlie and Janie, Jack and Claire—everybody has stopped by and sent their best wishes.

"Bill, Mr. Johnson has been here every single day as well as people from your work, Sarah and Rosie and others. They have all stopped by to check on you, and we've held prayer sessions here in the room every night for the past three days with the kids. Everyone asking God to put his hand on you. Thank God, he has heard our prayers!"

CeCe's voice is cracking badly, but she can't stop talking. I know she is truly grateful that I am conscious. And I am grateful that she is here and that I am not dead—yet, anyway! She can talk all she wants; I am just glad to hear her voice.

CeCe cradles my head and gives me a soft kiss on the cheek. "You had me worried, but you are going to be all right. I just know it!"

I smile at her and my eyes start well up with tears. Yes, thank God. I am a lucky man, for sure!

As the next few days pass, CeCe stays right by my side, sleeping in the convertible chair in the room. I receive so many visitors, and outside of CeCe and my kids, there is no more visitor more important than Detective Higgins who also frequently checked in on me while I was unconscious.

As I slowly begin to regain my memory of the events of that night, little pieces are coming back to me but not all at once. Up until then, I can only recall small details every now and then, but it isn't until Detective Higgins's visit about a week later that I am given the sequence of events that occurred. Detective Higgins helps me piece the events together of what happened that put me where I am now, and then I had a clear understanding of the ordeal and most importantly, why.

Evidently, Maria Milken was determined to take my life that night. She had killed Alice Randle in the employee parking lot on that fateful Monday evening earlier in the week. She had found out about John's affair with Alice and she had written the note left on Alice's doorstep the previous weekend. John must have felt like Maria was getting suspicious so he had confronted Alice in his office earlier on the night prior to the shooting. He told her that they had to end the relationship, but she was not having any part of it, and the argument in his office ensued, which was witnessed by several of the night warehouse personnel.

After John left the warehouse for the evening, he went home, which was his normal routine. He followed his regular routine going to sleep around 10:00 p.m. before coming back in early the next day. In order to cover the warehouse operations as instructed, Alice had been scheduling herself in to work around five in the afternoon and worked until three or four in the morning before heading for home. She had someone staying with her children through the evenings until she arrived back home in the early hours and was then there for them when they woke in the morning. She got them off to daycare and kindergarten and then returned home to catch up on her sleep, waking to be there when they got back home.

On occasion, John would make up a reason to tell Maria he needed to come into the warehouse earlier than normal. Instead, he would meet Alice at the Radisson Hotel about two blocks from work. Detective Higgins had suspected there must have been a pattern to their infidelity so he had checked camera recordings for all the hotels within a five-mile radius of the warehouse and easily uncovered the clandestine meetings between the two. On the night of the shooting and after John had fallen asleep, Maria had taken John's truck, driven to the warehouse parking lot, and waited for Alice to come out to her car in the employee parking lot. She was smart enough to know that, if seen, John's truck would not be viewed as unusual in ODI's parking lot.

Higgins believes that Maria had originally intended to just scare Alice away from John by threatening her with the showing of a gun. Obviously, the confrontation escalated into an altercation between the two women, and Maria's deep hatred for Alice caused by her husband's infidelity with this younger woman prompted her to shoot and kill Alice in response. She returned home before John was awakened by the phone call from the night supervisor informing him of the shooting in the parking lot. He immediately left for the warehouse and arrived just as the paramedics were leaving to transport Alice to the hospital. His anxiety and anger directed toward me when Sarah had handed him her cell phone as I was driving in to work that night was heightened by his suspicion and realization that his wife may have been the person responsible for shooting Alice. Of course, he was going to try and cover for her as best he could and is precisely why he would not admit to Detective Higgins about the affair with Alice. Admitting to the affair with Alice would certainly thrust Maria into the role of an angry wife and a prime suspect.

According to Higgins, John has now admitted that he had suspected that his wife may have been Alice's killer. However, he claims that he did not ever confront her about it and that she never told him that she was the one who killed Alice. Of course, it would be insane of him to admit to knowing she was the killer and risk the possibility of being charged with aiding in the cover-up of a crime, or even worse, contributing in some way to the death of Alice Randle. He also claims to have had no knowledge of Alice's intention to offer herself sexually to me in an attempt to obtain ODI's support. Maria had panicked when she found out John was being questioned at police headquarters as she was sure she would eventually be suspected if John admitted to the affair. When Maria came to see me and offer herself for sexual favors, Detective Higgins believes she had every intention on following through with her offer. In her mind, with ODI's support, this might get the police to turn attention away from John and possibly start to look elsewhere for Alice's killer. In addition, if I had taken her up on the offer, it would become her ultimate revenge in getting back at John for his infidelity. In her mind, it would be poetic justice to have sexual relations with the man John despised most. Evidently, it was clear to Maria that John and I were not on best terms, which was apparent to most everyone who knew the both of us.

Okay, so everything is coming clear to me, but there is one thing I do not know and has not been explained yet. If Maria is the one who killed Alice and then attempted to shoot me, where is she? What happened to Maria? Is she under arrest? Did she flee the scene? Is a fugitive from justice? Detective Higgins must have that answer for sure!

Detective explains that after catching up to Maria and talking with her in Sarah's office on that day following her proposition to me in my office, he became suspicious that she was the killer and had purposefully staged the scene in my office by posing as the victim when I refused to go along. She hoped that I would go for the bait and then hoped to have ODI intervene with the police since John had told her that as the HR Director, I was working with the police on the investigation. When I did not fall for her scheme, she quickly improvised by turning the tables on me by claiming that it was I who propositioned her, seeing an opportunity to take advantage of a desperate wife merely trying to support her husband. Higgins was not buying it as it was obvious that her attire on that day was really over the top. "Who arrives for a serious meeting with a company official dressed like she was going to the club?" he had asked himself. That started him thinking that she had an ulterior motive for requesting the audience with me. He said that one of the questions he asked her in Sarah's office was, how she thought getting a letter of support from ODI would benefit her husband. When she stuttered and then tried to change the subject, he realized that the episode in my office was phony, and this woman might be more of a suspect than her husband, especially if the affair with Alice was true. It also then that he brought the letter left on Alice's doorstep into play. Yes, the letter…that would connect Maria directly to the affair between Alice and John.

"Okay, sure, that gives her reason and motive for killing Alice, but why did she believe that killing me was necessary? I was not the person who suspected her of killing Alice," I ask Higgins.

Higgins goes on to explain that she needed something else to support her claim of sexual harassment against me. She thought if she could stage an accident showing that it was I who followed her from the ODI parking lot in an attempt to run her off the road, This would validate her claim that I had tried to take advantage of her when she came in to ask ODI for help for John since he had worked at for so long with the company. What she did not anticipate was the heavy traffic on the street when she followed me from the parking lot.

After his conversation with Maria, Higgins stayed in the ODI parking lot and from his unmarked car observed Maria when she exited the building after leaving Sarah's office. But when she drove out of the parking lot and then stopped outside the fence line alongside the road, Higgins thought that was odd. He decided to wait in his vehicle and observe while Maria sat in her parked car. When I exited the building, got in my car, and pulled out on to street leading out of the parking lot, he noticed that Maria flipped on her headlights and quickly fell in behind me in the right-hand lane, causing an approaching car to brake hard to miss hitting her. Higgins was convinced something was going down. I recall noticing this as well, but thought it was just another commuter anxious to get home, like me. Hey, this is the norm for driving almost anywhere these days—people in a hurry to get somewhere.

Higgins then explains that he realized that she had been waiting for me to leave so he drove out of the ODI parking lot to follow us both and continue surveillance. Unfortunately, the traffic was so heavy that he had to wait before he could exit onto the street and could only get as close as ten cars behind her car. He did not want to alert her to his presence therefore he did not turn on his police lights to stop traffic, which would have allowed him to exit the parking lot more quickly. However, when he noticed she was tailgating me, he knew she was attempting to create a dangerous situation and he could no longer stay back and watch.

He maneuvered his police car through the heavy traffic but could only get as close as four cars behind her vehicle. However, when he weaved over into the left-hand lane, his car became blocked from the traffic stop ahead of him. That's when he noticed that I had suddenly braked and gone off the road to the right. All he could do was pull over to the left, exit his vehicle, and run toward my car. He got there but didn't see me because I had already turned and ran behind my vehicle. That's when he saw Maria running against the traffic, and he took off after her.

"So, why did she feel like it was necessary to shoot at me if she was trying to establish it was me who was following her?" I ask.

Higgins says that because I pulled over to the right so quickly, she could not brake as fast and had no choice but to go past my parked car and then slam on brakes, stopping thirty feet ahead. He goes on to say that Maria was a highly emotionally unstable person, and when she felt threatened or challenged, her anger overcame her mental stability, and just like with Alice, she reacted with me in the same way. Her instinct was to hurt me, and the only way for her to satisfy this inner anger was to shoot the person who she perceived was the cause.

"Okay, but she did shoot me, and I'm damn lucky to be alive. What happened to her then?" I inquire.

Higgins looks down at the floor for a moment and then says that he wishes that he had recognized her intention sooner and if so, he would have most definitely intervened right when she began to follow me but he had no indication that she planned to shoot me. He goes on to explain that as he approached, he noticed Maria standing in front of me about ten feet away raising her right arm to shoot. He stopped, pulled his service weapon, and yelled, "Stop, police!"

When she ignored his demand, he fired his gun, but it was just a split second after she had already pulled the trigger on the .22 revolver she had in her hand. He saw Maria collapse to the pavement as the shot from his .45 auto found its mark, right into the lower base of her brain. She was pronounced dead at the scene. He ran over to where I lay, already unconscious from her shot to my right chest, and attempted to revive me and applying pressure to my profusely bleeding gunshot wound. He immediately radioed for medical assistance on his two-way cell phone.

Detective Higgins's actions to fire his service weapon and apply pressure to my chest wound more than likely saved my life according to the attending doctor and the investigating state attorney's office findings. Officer Higgins is awarded the Meritorious Service Medal for saving a citizen's life in the line of duty in a ceremony that I was, fortunately, able to attend in a wheelchair a few months later.

Over the next few weeks, I slowly regain my strength and even start rehabilitation to build my stamina and coordination. The attending doctor has been in regularly to check on my progress. He has been optimistic about my recovery and said the reason I was unconscious for three days was due to the severe trauma my body experienced and was not uncommon, but that my vital signs were always trending positive. I know one thing for sure, I will not be leaving this hospital for a while yet and then the real work will begin for me. I learn later that apparently, my heart had stopped beating twice on the way to the hospital after passing out on that roadway. Thanks to the paramedics with the Metro Fire Department, I was successfully revived and taken right into surgery to remove the bullet that pierced the right side of my chest, collapsing the lung, and coming to rest lodged next to my spine. It was within a quarter inch from impacting the spinal cord which would've surely cause paralysis if it had. Obviously, I lost a lot of blood from the bullet wound and road rash and was administered two quarts of blood transfusions. My left leg was broken in two places and had to be surgically repaired in order to adequately set the bone for healing. Apparently, I was running so fast that when I hit that car door, my femur was shattered upon impact. It will be quite a while before I will be able to walk normally again. I will have several weeks of transitional rehabilitation in front of me, with the ultimate goal of being able to walk without a limp or with the use of an artificial device. First things first though, my chest and lung need to heal before I can even think about working on walking. However, that doesn't keep my day nurse, Steph, from coming in every two hours to stretch the leg where my femur was broken in two places. She claims the doctor ordered this to prevent the bone from setting too tightly which might affect my ability to walk in a normal manner at a later date. I'm not sure, but this kind of sounds "made-up" to me…especially when Steph has this sly smile on her face as she bends my knee back and forth to stretch the quad muscle and ham string…YEOH, that hurts so bad! I can't help but think of her as the mean head nurse in the movie "One Flew Over the Cuckoo's Nest," starring Jack Nicholson where she antagonized his character at every turn to show him who was really in charge. Yep, Steph has become my "Nurse Ratched," and you know what? I think she really likes the comparison which is surprising since from the get together with her and her husband, Dave. I thought she was a friend! At least get the smile off your face when you inflict that kind of pain on me…not funny! Based on the most recent tests and evaluation, the doctor says, even at my age, I have a decent chance at a full recovery. However, I sincerely believe I will fully recover because, you see, I have always been fortunate. Considering the alternatives, my life has been blessed beyond my wildest dreams, and most importantly, I have the most wonderful partner I could ever have! CeCe has been by my side every single day and most nights in my hospital room bringing her laptop so as not to get behind on her work. Since I doze off frequently with the steady drip of pain medication in my IV, she has plenty of opportunity…and I was under the impression a shot of bourbon was the only magic elixir I could rely on!

During the first few weeks in the hospital, many team members from Ocean Direct stop in to visit, all passing on their best wishes for a speedy recovery and of course wanting to hear first hand from me the events of that fateful evening. I guess most people don't believe what they hear from someone else, so they have this strange need to get it directly from the person involved. Or maybe, they think it's good for the afflicted to talk about an ordeal that almost ended their life, you know, like helping them obtain closure and get it behind them, kind of like some sort of therapy, so to speak. Hmmm…I can honestly tell you that after about the tenth time I was asked to explain exactly what happened, I was less than enthusiastic about reliving this experience…any longer! But I bit my tongue and held my frustration inside. I accommodated each request with a genuinely forced smile, answering each follow-up question and leaving out no detail. When my boss, Carl Johnson, stopped in to visit a couple of days after surgery, he was quite explicit about me getting my tail back to work as soon as possible since there were rumors beginning to surface that we might now have a drug ring operating on the premises. Christ, you take a few days off to recover from gunshot wounds and everything at work falls apart. Guess I should take it as a positive sign that my expertise is still in demand; for sure none of those spineless senior managers are chomping at the bit to tackle a possible drug ring issue! Although, I could certainly envision Sam Morris stepping up to take charge like instituting a curfew, proclaiming everything is under control, or issuing some other "hey, I'm in charge" order. So, that being said, Carl informs me that I only have one month before he begins daily Zoom meetings, with my mandatory participation, of course. Nice to know you're needed…right?

As I think about what has happened over the last week of my life, it dawns on me that maybe I've been asking myself the wrong damn question. Instead of asking when will I be "getting to the end" perhaps better questions would be, "what the hell's next and will I really make it?" After all, I still have two more years of this circus fun house to get through! I can hardly wait to find out what is next, as I shift my position in bed and a painful reminder that the next few weeks will be challenging enough shoots down my hip…so for now, Ocean Direct will just have to wait. I have more important issues on my plate! But I still can't help thinking that what I lived through this past week is nothing compared to what lies ahead… God almighty, what I'd give right now to have a Four Roses, neat! Yeah, like that's going to happen, not with the beloved psycho nurse from the movie, One Flew Over the Cuckoo's Nest Nurse Ratched on the job.

"Getting to the End."

About the Author

Michael Willis has spent most of his career in the human resources field, having served for more than forty years with various *Fortune 500* organizations, private companies, and a municipal government entity. His last full-time employment was vice president of human resources for a family-owned retail, warehousing, and construction company. He possesses a bachelor of arts degree with an emphasis in industrial relations from the University of South Florida and has also earned a Certificate of Senior Professional in Human Resources from the Society for Human Resource Management (SHRM). Keeping a connection to the HR world, Michael is presently engaged as a senior VP with a renowned human resources consulting firm. His human resources expertise, particularly in the employee relations discipline, has provided him with the knowledge, training, and impetus for writing this book, the contents of which are purely fictitious, having no reference to actual people, places, or real events (*ahem, lawyers advise this type of disclosure to protect the innocent. Wait, what? Okay, we get it, you just can't make this stuff up*).

Michael grew up in Florida, relocating from North Carolina at a young age with his parents and three siblings. He currently resides in Central Florida, staying connected with his sisters and brother, spending leisure time outdoors, and enjoying fishing, boating, and biking. He has been blessed with four very talented children, successful within their own right, and is the quintessential proud grandfather to three amazing grandkids.

CPSIA information can be obtained
at www.ICGtesting.com
Printed in the USA
JSHW022044121122
33064JS00001B/58